East of the Sun and West of the Moon

Twenty-One Norwegian Folk Tales

These tales have been adapted from the

Dasent Translation

of the Collection of Asbjörnsen and Moe

East of the Sun
and West of the Moon

Twenty-One Norwegian Folk Tales

Edited and Illustrated by

Ingri and Edgar Parin d'Aulaire

THE JUNIOR LITERARY GUILD
CORPORATION
AND
NEW YORK · THE VIKING PRESS · MCMXXXIX

FIRST PUBLISHED OCTOBER 1938
COPYRIGHT 1938 BY INGRI AND EDGAR PARIN D'AULAIRE
PRINTED IN U. S. A. PUBLISHED BY THE VIKING PRESS, INC.
COMPOSED IN FOURTEEN POINT JANSON TYPE BY THE COMPOSING ROOM, INC.
PRINTED AND BOUND BY THE STRATFORD PRESS. ILLUSTRATIONS PRINTED
BY THE GRAVURE PROCESS BY DUENEWALD PRINTING CORPORATION
DISTRIBUTED IN CANADA BY THE MACMILLAN COMPANY OF CANADA, LTD.

About Norway and These Tales

Between the little houses and huts that lie scattered across the hilly and rocky land of Norway, there are wide stretches of deep forests and blue mountains. For days you can wander about without meeting another human being, and all unaware you step into a strange fairy-tale world. Across the bogs glide shapes of mist like grey, woolly gnomes. On a ridge stands the dried-up trunk of a tree, its thin branches straggling like scrawny troll-hag arms; and its head is tucked in under one of them. In the distance the sun breaks through drifting clouds, and shines on a small hillock far down in the valley. It beams and glitters like the golden castle East of the Sun and West of the Moon.

Near by stands a cracked and weathered stone, and you don't even need imagination to see that it is one of those trolls that turned around and looked into the rising sun, which is the end of all trolls. A black form sticks out of the foaming water in the middle of the fall. That is the Sprite of the Waterfall, who sits there playing sadly on his fiddle; and the fine little tune you hear so thinly vibrating through the clear air, does it come from his fiddle or from the falling water?

Something rustles and creaks in the wood. You can't be sure it isn't the Hulder, the beautiful Hill-Maid with golden braids and a cow's tail, who walks through the forest scheming to get herself a Christian for a husband, for if she can her soul too will be eternal.

In the quiet closed-in valleys of Norway the tales of these hill-folk and forest-sprites, of trolls with nine heads and kings with golden crowns, have flourished. And always it is the lazy but cunning lad who by his wit triumphs over all, and gets the beautiful princess and half the kingdom. From generation to generation these tales were told in a tradition-bound and almost fixed form. The coming of newspapers and modern industrial life would have caused this age-old art to be lost for ever had not Peter Christen Asbjörnsen and Jörgen Moe just in the nick of time understood the value of the old tales and set out to collect them. The effect of these tales on modern Norwegian literature, from Ibsen down, is immeasurable. Asbjörnsen was the son of a glazier in Oslo, Moe the son of a well-to-do farmer; Asbjörnsen a zoologist and forester, Moe a poet and a bishop. They had met in their boyhood. As young students they started independently of each other to collect tales among the country people, and when one day they found out that they were both working on the same thing, they joined forces with great enthusiasm and swore eternal friendship, sealing it in a romantic gesture by letting their blood flow together. And this friendship lasted all through their lives.

Asbjörnsen's was the vigorous temperament, Moe's had the poetic charm. In their first collections, which were published in the early forties, one easily distinguishes the work of the one from the other, but later they had learned so much from each other that their style became nearly identical. They published one little volume of fairy-tales after the other, raising strong protest from the conservatives, who thought that these tales smacked too much of the soil. But the two collectors took this criticism calmly, answered it with ridicule, and went on with their work. They found their way to strange and rarely gifted story tellers who lived in small log cabins deep in the forests, old peasants who sat there in the flickering light of their fireplaces, dressed in leather breeches and peasant blouses, telling their tales in the straightforward language of the valley. Moe describes one of these story tellers who was fitted out with four lips, a big scar from a fight with a bear, and but one eye, which had the life of two. The words fell out richer and fuller from his grotesque hare-mouth than from any ordinary mouth; he didn't talk with half a mouth, not nicely and sweetly for the ears of the delicate town ladies of that time. And faithfully Asbjörnsen and Moe kept the intensity of the language and the strength and boldness of the tales.

In the late 1850's the Englishman George Webbe Dasent, upon the suggestion of the German fairy-tale collector Jacob Grimm, began to translate these Norwegian folk tales into English. Though his first translations were still entirely bound by the English mode of thinking, not even printing the names of the two Norwegian collectors on the title page, he soon translated most of the tales, and later editions are so excellent that many of his terms have become established in the Norwegian-English dictionaries. Through the eighty years that have passed since Dasent began his translations, many writers have made new translations; but none of them bears comparison with his.

When we started to make our selection from the nearly hundred fairy tales, we planned to do a translation of our own. But after working on it for a while we saw that it would be senseless to try just to make a different translation from Dasent's nearly perfect version; that is, with respect to language. But his typically Victorian and English conceptions in many passages disturbed us much, and here and there misunderstandings had crept in through too literal rendering, as when the lovely Norwegian maiden "tosses the other suitor out through the window," instead of "throwing him over, jilting him, and taking the right one in his place." So, finally, with an old Norwegian edition, Dasent's translation, and our own translation, we worked through the stories word by word. Of two of the tales, however, we had to make an entirely new translation; Dasent's translations of "Herding the King's Hares," our favourite among all the tales, and of the "Ship That Went As Well by Land As by Sea," were to be found only in a very early edition and had kept very little of the Norwegian original. We hope that nobody will find that we have committed sacrilege in correcting and editing the master. Times have changed, and while Dasent had more mastery of the English language than we do, we not only have a greater command of the Norwegian language but also of the different dialect expressions that are the life of these stories; and, above all, we have been imbued with the spirit and language of these tales since the time we learned to talk, and they are not to us mere philological exercises, but naturally have one of the softest spots in our hearts.

The most difficult work we had with this edition was to pick out

About Norway and These Tales

these twenty-one stories. It was as if parents had to pick out among their hundred children the ones they thought the most of, though, good and bad, they loved them all. Actually nearly all the tales are built up around a dozen-odd themes, differently combined and in different settings, but as to form no two are alike. It is as if each theme were given many faces. Some of the tales have strong affinities to tales from England, Germany, and other countries, and these we left out. Then we arranged the rest in groups, selecting the ones we thought the most typical within each group. But occasionally within the same group two of the tales were so beautiful that we didn't have the heart to leave out either one.

Even the selection of the illustrations was difficult, and we should have liked to have made five times as many drawings. The tales were charmingly illustrated at the end of the last century by some of the best Norwegian artists, but these drawings are so delicate, and so subtly Norwegian, that only Norwegians can truly understand them. Those who do not know Norway cannot feel the meaning of the sharp silhouette of a tree top against a golden summer-night sky—the mist shapes that rise from the bog. So illustrations must be translated as well as words. Our aim here has been to find the middle road, that those who are brought up on these stories in their native surroundings may say that they are true, indeed, and that those who do not know Norway will also find the right meaning in them.

We have a little farm in Norway that lies far up on the hillside, deep in the forest, with the bare mountains towering straight above it. Far down in the valley, miles and miles away, you can see a few little lights twinkling in the night. They are the only signs of human beings. And up here in the loneliness we lived during the light summer, during the clear, sparkling fall, during the dark winter, when the light of the moon glittered on the snow, and here we walked around in forest and fields and made the sketches for these illustrations.

I. AND E. P. D'A.

New York,
July 1938

Contents

Illustrations

East of the Sun and West of the Moon

Twenty-One Norwegian Folk Tales

Herding the King's Hares

ONCE there was a farmer who had turned over his farm to his oldest son. But he had three more sons; their names were Per, Paal, and Espen Cinderlad. They stayed at home with their father and wouldn't do a thing, for they fared too well. And they thought themselves too good for anything, and nothing was good enough for them.

But then, at long last, it came to Per's ears that the king wanted a shepherd to herd his hares, and so he told his father that that was where he wanted to go, that was just the thing for him. He would serve no less a man than the king himself. The old man thought there might be some work that would suit him better. The one who was to herd hares had to be lithe and light on his feet and no sleepy-head, for, when the hares began to gad and scud, it would be quite another dance than pottering around on the floors at home.

Well, that couldn't be helped. Per would go there and he must go there. So he put his knapsack on his back and trudged down the hill, and when he had walked far and farther than far, he came to an old hag whose nose had got caught in a log of wood. And when he saw how she pulled and tore to get loose, he began to roar with laughter.

"Don't stand there grinning," said the old hag, "but come and help a poor body. I was going to chop up some firewood when my nose got caught in a crack, and so I have been standing here, pulling and jerking, and haven't tasted a bit of food for a hundred years," she said.

But Per just laughed still more. He thought it only funny. If she had been standing like that for a hundred years, she could certainly bear it for another hundred, he said.

When he came to the king's farm, he at once got the job as shepherd.

Herding the King's Hares

It wasn't hard to get work there. Good food and good pay he should have, and perhaps he would even get the king's daughter in the bargain. But if as much as one of the king's hares got lost, the king would cut three red strips off his back, and throw him into the snake pit.

Well, as long as Per stayed in the lane between the fields and in the cattle run, the hares stayed all in one flock. But as the day went on and they came up into the woods, the hares began to scamper and gad about all over the hills. Per hurried after them. As long as there was one in sight he ran for all he was worth. When the last one had disappeared and he had almost raced himself to death, he saw no more of them. Late in the afternoon he began to stroll homewards, and stopped at the pasture gate, gaping and gazing around for the hares. But no, there didn't come as much as a single hare, and when he got to the king's hall in the evening, the king was standing with his knife ready, and cut three red strips from his back, sprinkled salt and pepper on it, and then into the snake pit with him.

After a while Paal was the one who wanted to set off and herd the king's hares. The old man said the same to him, and even a little more than that. But he would go and he must go, it just couldn't be helped. And it went neither better nor worse with him than it had gone with Per.

The old hag was standing there pulling and jerking with her nose caught in the log, and he laughed and thought it only funny and let her stay there and wriggle.

Work he got on the spot; he didn't get no for an answer. But the hares scudded and scattered all over the hills. It didn't help a bit that he ran for all he was worth in the broiling sun, till he puffed and panted like a shepherd's dog. And when he came home to the king's hall in the evening without a hare, the king was standing there in the courtyard with his knife ready, and cut three strips from his back, sprinkled it with salt and pepper, and then into the snake pit with him.

By and by Cinderlad wanted to be off and herd the king's hares, and told the old man about it. He thought it would be just the right kind of work for him to slip around in the woods and fields and strawberry

grounds, and to ramble about after a flock of hares, and to take naps on the sunny hillsides in between, he said.

The old man thought there might be some other kind of work that would suit him better, for if he didn't fare worse, he certainly wouldn't fare better than his brothers. The one who was to herd the king's hares mustn't stomp about like a sleepy-head with leaden socks on his feet, or like a louse on a tarstick; for when the hares began to gad about on the sunny hillsides, it would be at least as bad as trying to catch fleas with mittens on. The one who was to get away from that with a whole back had to be more than lithe and light on his feet, and leap and run he must, faster than a dried skin or a bird's wing.

Well, that couldn't be helped, said Espen Cinderlad, he would go to the king's farm to serve the king, for no lesser man would he serve, he said. And the hares he would certainly know how to herd, they couldn't be so much worse than the goat and the calf.

Then Cinderlad put his knapsack on his back and trudged down the hill. When he had gone far and farther than far, so that he began to get good and hungry, he came to the old hag who was standing with her nose in the log of wood, pulling and jerking and trying to get loose.

"Good day, Granny," he said. "Are you standing here sharpening your nose, you poor old soul?"

"Oh, but nobody has called me Granny for a hundred years," said the old hag. "Come now and help me to get loose and give me something to eat, for I have had no food in my mouth during all that time, and I'll do you a good turn again for that," she said.

Yes, then she might well need both food and drink, said Espen Cinderlad.

Then he split the log for her so she got her nose out of the crack, and he shared his food with her, and they sat down to eat. The old hag had no lack of appetite, you may be sure, so she took the lion's share of the food.

When they had finished, she gave Cinderlad a whistle and told him how to use it. If he blew it from one end, the things which he wanted to get rid of would scatter to all sides, and when he blew it from the other end, they would all come back again. If the whistle was lost or was taken from him, he had only to wish for it and it would come back to him.

"That was some whistle," thought Espen Cinderlad.

When he came to the king's farm, he at once was hired as a shepherd. It wasn't hard to get work there, and food and good pay he should have. And if he was able to herd the king's hares so not one was lost, he might perhaps even get the king's daughter. But if any got away, even one of the tiniest hares, they were to cut three red strips from his back, and the king was so sure of this that he went straight over and sharpened his knife then and there.

"It will be easy enough to herd these hares," thought Espen Cinderlad, for when they were let out of the stable they were almost as tame as a flock of sheep, and as long as they stayed in the lane between the fields and in the cattle run, he had them all in a flock. But when they reached the woody slope towards noontime, and the sun began to glare and broil on clearings and slopes, they began to scatter and gad about all over the hills.

"Hey-day, eya! Off you go," cried Espen Cinderlad, and blew the whistle from one end, and off they went to all the corners of the world, and out of sight. But when he came to a green glade where once there had been a charcoal kiln, he blew the whistle from the other end, and in the jerk of a lamb's tail all the hares were back and stood lined up in rows and ranks, so he could look them over like a troop of soldiers on the drill-ground.

"This is some whistle," thought Espen.

Then he went to sleep on a sunny hillside, and the hares scudded about and took care of themselves. Towards evening he whistled them together again and led them back to the king's hall just like a flock of sheep.

The king and the queen and the princess, too, stood in the doorway

and wondered what kind of fellow this might be, who could herd the hares so well that he brought them home again.

The king counted and counted the hares, and pointed with his finger and counted again, but there wasn't so much as a leveret missing.

"What a boy!" said the princess.

The next day he went to the woods to herd again. But as he was lazing about in the strawberry field, up came the chambermaid of the king's hall. She was to try to find out how it happened that he could herd the king's hares so well.

Well, he pulled out the whistle and showed it to her, and then he blew into one end so the hares scattered like the wind over hills and dales, and then he blew into the other end and the hares came trotting back to the strawberry field and lined up there in rows and ranks again.

That was a strange whistle, thought the chambermaid. She would gladly give a hundred dollars for it if he would sell it, she said.

Yes, that was some whistle, said Espen Cinderlad. It wasn't for sale for money, but if she would give him two hundred dollars and a kiss for each dollar, then she could have it, he said.

Oh, yes, that she would gladly do, she would willingly give him two for each one, and many thanks in the bargain.

So she got the whistle; but when she arrived at the king's hall the whistle had gone, for Espen Cinderlad had wished it back again. And towards evening he came home with his hares again, they trotted along like a flock of sheep, and for all that the king counted and pointed, it didn't help. He could not find so much as a hair of them missing.

The third day he was out herding, they sent the princess out to try to get the whistle away from him. She made herself as sweet as sugar and as gay as a lark, and then she offered him two hundred dollars if he would sell her the whistle and tell her how to behave to get it safe home.

"Yes, it certainly is some whistle," said Espen Cinderlad, and it wasn't for sale, he said. But that was all the same, he would have to sell it for her sake. If she would give him the two hundred dollars and a kiss in

18

the bargain for each dollar, then she could have the whistle. And if she wanted to keep it, she had to watch it well—that was her business.

That was a high price for a hare-whistle, thought the princess, and it went a little against the grain to give him the kisses. But as they were in the wood so nobody could either see or hear it, she would have to let it go, for the whistle she must have, she said. And when Espen Cinderlad had got what he was to have, she got the whistle, and she kept it tightly pressed in her hand all the way home. But when she arrived at the hall and wanted to show it, it had vanished from between her fingers.

The next day the queen would go herself and try to get the whistle from him, and she was quite sure she would bring it back with her too.

She was more stingy with the dollars, and didn't offer him more than fifty, but she had to raise her price till at last it was three hundred. Cinderlad said it was some whistle and that it was a ridiculous bid. But for her sake he had to let it pass; if she would give him three hundred dollars and a smacking kiss for each dollar she could have it. Of that he got full measure, for she wasn't stingy in that.

When she had got the whistle, she tied it up and hid it too. But she had no better luck than the others, for when she wanted to pull it out and show it, the whistle had vanished. And in the evening Espen Cinderlad came home driving his hares like a flock of tame sheep.

"Stuff and nonsense," said the king. "I'll have to go myself if we are to get this confounded whistle away from him."

So when Espen Cinderlad had gone to the woods with the hares the next day, the king set out after him and caught up with him on the same sunny hillside where the women folk had made their bargains with him. Yes, they were great friends and agreed about everything, and Espen showed him the whistle and let him hold it, and blew it, first in one end and then in the other. And the king thought it a very strange whistle and wanted by all means to buy it.

"Yes, it certainly is some whistle," said Espen Cinderlad, "but it isn't for sale for money. But do you see the white mare that stands there in the bog beside the great fir-tree?" he said.

"Yes, that is my own horse, that is Whitey," said the king. He knew that himself without anybody telling him.

"Well, if you'll give me a thousand dollars and kiss Whitey, you shall have the whistle."

"Isn't it for sale at any other price?" asked the king.

"No, it isn't," said Espen Cinderlad.

"Well, but I take it that you'll let me put my silk handkerchief between?" said the king.

That he might do. And so he got the whistle and put it in his purse, and the purse he put in his pocket, and the pocket he buttoned well. But when he arrived at his house and wanted to pull out the whistle, he was no better off than the women folk. He had no more whistle to show than they had. And Espen Cinderlad came driving the hares home and not a hair of them was missing.

The king was in a great rage that Cinderlad had fooled them all and had cheated him, too, out of the whistle. Now Cinderlad should lose his life, there was no question about that. 'Twas always best to have such a rogue out of the play, the sooner the better.

Espen Cinderlad said this was neither just nor justice, he had only done what they wanted him to do; and so he had saved his back and his life as well as he could. "Well, never mind that," said the king. "If you can tell so many lies that they fill the big brewing-vat so that it overflows, your life shall be spared," he said.

That was neither a hard nor a long task, said Espen Cinderlad. He thought well he could master that job. And so he began to tell how things had happened right from the beginning. He told about the old hag with her nose in the log of wood, and every now and then he threw in: "I have to think up some lies, if the vat is to get filled." Then he talked about the whistle which he had got, about the chambermaid who came to him and wanted to buy it for a hundred dollars and about all

the kisses she had to give in the bargain over there on the sunny hill-side. And then he talked about the princess, how she came to him and kissed him so well to get the whistle, because nobody could see or hear it over there in the woods. "I have to tell a lot of lies, if the vat is to get filled," said Espen Cinderlad. Then he talked about the queen, how stingy she was with her dollars and how generous she was with her smacks. "I have to tell a lot of lies, if the vat is to get filled," said Espen Cinderlad.

"I think it's getting pretty full now," said the king.

"Oh, no," said the queen.

Then he began to talk about the king who came to him, and about the white mare down in the bog, and if he wanted the whistle he had to—he had to——

"Yes, with your permission I have to tell a whole lot of lies, if the vat is to get filled," said Espen Cinderlad.

"Wait, wait. It is filled, lad. Don't you see it is flowing over?" cried the king.

Then the king and queen thought it best to give him the princess and half the kingdom; it just couldn't be helped.

"That certainly was some whistle," said Espen Cinderlad.

The Ship That Went As Well by Land As by Sea

ONCE upon a time there was a king, and this king had heard about a ship that went just as well by land as by sea. So he set his heart on having one like that too, and promised his daughter and half the kingdom to the one who could build such a ship for him. And this he had cried out from all the church-hills in his realm. There were many who tried, you may be sure; for I suppose they thought they would like well to have half the kingdom, and to get the king's daughter into the bargain wouldn't be so bad either. But they all fared badly.

Now there were three brothers who lived in a far-away parish deep in the woods. The eldest was called Per, the second was called Paal, and the youngest was called Espen Cinderlad, because he always sat in the hearth poking and raking in the ashes. But on the Sunday when it was cried out about the ship which the king wished to have, it so happened that Cinderlad had moved out of the hearth and had gone to church. When he came home and told what he had heard, Per, who was the eldest, asked his mother to get some food ready for him, for now he was going away to try if he could build the ship and win the king's daughter and half the kingdom.

So he put the bag with food on his back and set out. When he had walked for a while, he met an old man who was so very crooked and decrepit.

The Ship That Went As Well by Land As by Sea

"Where are you going?" asked the man.

"I am going to the forest to make a trough for my father. He won't eat from the family dish," said Per.

"Trough it shall be," said the man. "What do you have in your bag?"

"Dung," answered Per.

"Dung it shall be," said the man.

Then Per went over to the great oak-forest and began to saw and hammer, and work away as hard as he could. But as much as he sawed and as much as he chopped, and as hard as he tried to make a ship, he could turn out only troughs and nothing but troughs. Towards noon he wanted a bit to eat, and opened his bag. But what he found in his bag certainly wasn't food! So, as he had nothing to eat and as he didn't turn out anything but troughs, he got tired of the work, took the ax and the bag on his shoulder, and went home to his mother again.

Then Paal wanted to set out and try his luck at building the ship and winning the princess and half the kingdom. He asked his mother for some food and, when the bag was ready, he threw it over his shoulder and set out towards the woods. When he had walked for a while he met an old man who was so very crooked and decrepit.

"Where are you going?" said the man.

"Oh, I am going into the forest to make a trough for our sucking-pig," said Paal.

"Pig trough it shall be," said the man. "What have you got in your bag?" asked the man.

"Dung," said Paal.

"Dung it shall be," said the man.

Then Paal went to the wood and began to saw and chop and hew, and he worked as hard as he could, but no matter how he cut and how he put the pieces together, everything he made turned out to be pig troughs. In spite of this he didn't give up, but worked away till late in the afternoon before he even thought of food. Then all of a sudden he got so hungry that he had to hurry and open his food bag, but there wasn't a bit of *food* in the bag. Then he got so mad that he turned the

The Ship That Went As Well by Land As by Sea

bag inside out and struck it against a stump of a tree, picked up his tools, and set off for home.

As soon as Paal got home, Cinderlad wanted to set out, and he asked his mother for a bag of food. "Perhaps I might be able to build the ship and win the princess and half the kingdom," he said.

"Sure, sure," said his mother, "you who never do a thing but sit in the fireplace and rake the ashes. No, you certainly won't get a bag of food."

But Cinderlad didn't give in for all that; he kept on begging and nagging so long that at last he got leave to go. But he didn't get any food to take along, oh, no, not at all. So he waited till his mother turned her back, and helped himself to a couple of oatmeal cakes and a drop of stale beer, and then he set out. When he had walked for a while, he met the old man who was so very crooked and decrepit and good for nothing.

"Where are you going?" said the man.

"Oh, I am bound for the woods, if so might be, to build a ship that goes as well by land as by sea," said Cinderlad; "for the king has promised that the one who can build such a ship shall have the princess and half the kingdom."

"What do you have in your bag?" asked the man.

"Oh, not much to talk about. It is supposed to be some food for my trip," answered Cinderlad.

"If you'll give me a little of your food I'll help you," said the man.

"Gladly," said Cinderlad. "But there is nothing in my bag but two oatmeal cakes and a drop of stale beer."

That didn't matter, said the man, if he only got a little, he would help him in return.

When they came to an old oak in the woods, the old man said: "Now you must cut out a chip and then put the chip back in its place, and when you have done that, you can lie down and go to sleep for a while." Yes, Cinderlad did as he was told. He went to sleep, and in his sleep he thought he heard someone chopping and sawing and hammering and joining, but he couldn't wake up till the old man called him, and then the ship stood quite finished by the side of the old oak.

The Ship That Went As Well by Land As by Sea

"Now go on board and take with you everyone you meet on your way," said the old man. Yes, Espen Cinderlad thanked him for the ship, sailed off, and said he would remember to do as he was told.

When he had sailed for a while, he came up to a tall, skinny fellow, who was lying beside a crag eating rubble-stones.

"What sort of fellow are you, lying here feeding on rubble-stones?" said Cinderlad.

Well, he was so hungry for meat that he could never get his fill; that was why he had to eat rubble-stone, he said, and then he asked if he might go along with the ship.

"Yes, if you want to come along, get in," said Cinderlad.

Yes, that he would do, and he brought along some huge stones for food.

When they had sailed for a while, they came up to a man who was lying on a sunny slope sucking at a barrel bung.

"Who are you," said Espen Cinderlad, "and what is the good of lying there sucking at a bung?"

"Oh, when one hasn't got the barrel, one has to be content with the bung," said the man. "I am always so thirsty, I can never get enough beer and wine," he said, and then he asked if he might go along with the ship.

"Yes, if you want to come along, get in," said Cinderlad.

Yes, that he would, so he went on board and brought along the bung for his thirst.

When they had sailed awhile again, they came up to one who was lying with one ear to the ground listening.

"Who are you and what is the good of lying there on the ground listening?" said Espen Cinderlad.

"I am listening to the grass, for I have such good ears that I can hear the grass growing," said the man, and then he asked if he might go along in the ship. He didn't get no for an answer.

"If you want to come along, get in," said Cinderlad.

Yes, that he would do, and in he got, he too.

When they had sailed for a while again, they came up to one who stood taking aim with his gun.

26

The Ship That Went As Well by Land As by Sea

"Who are you and why are you standing there pointing your gun?" said Cinderlad.

"My eyesight is so strong that I can shoot and hit a thing right at the end of the world," said the man, and then he asked if he might go along in the ship.

"If you want to come along, get in," said Cinderlad.

Yes, that he would do, and so he got in.

When they had sailed for a while longer, they came up to a man who was jumping around on one foot, and to the other was tied seven ship's pound weights.

"Who are you," said Cinderlad, "and what is the good of jumping about on one leg with seven ship's pound weights tied on the other?"

"I am so light and run so fast," he answered, "that if I should run on both my legs, I would get to the end of the world in less than five minutes." And then he asked if he might go along in the ship.

"If you want to come along, get in," said Cinderlad.

Yes, that he would do, and he climbed on board and joined Cinderlad and his companions.

When they had sailed for a while again, they came up to one who was holding his mouth shut with his hand.

"Who are you," said Cinderlad, "and what is the good of standing there keeping your mouth shut with your hand?"

"Oh, I have seven summers and fifteeen winters in my body; so I have good reasons for keeping my mouth well shut, for if they all got out at once, they would make an end to the world right away," he said, and then he asked if he might go along in the ship.

"If you want to come along, get in," said Cinderlad.

Yes, that he wanted, and so he got into the ship with the others.

Then they sailed on for a long while, and at last they came to the king's hall.

Cinderlad went straight up to the king and said the ship stood all ready in the courtyard, and now he would like to have the princess as the king had promised.

The Ship That Went As Well by Land As by Sea

The king didn't like this any too well, for Cinderlad was not much to look at, all black and sooty as he was. And the king didn't care to give his daughter to such a tramp. So he told him to wait a bit, he couldn't get the princess till he had emptied his storehouse, which had three hundred barrels of meat in it. "That is all the same, if by this time tomorrow you have done it, you shall have her," said the king.

"I'll have to try," said Cinderlad, "but I suppose you don't mind if I take one of my companions along?"

No, that he could do; even all six of them if he wanted, said the king, for he thought it quite impossible even if he took six hundred with him.

Cinderlad took along only the one who ate stones and always was craving for meat. And when the people came to open the door of the storehouse, next day, he had eaten all the meat except six small smoked legs of mutton, one for each of his comrades. Then Cinderlad went straight to the king and said that now the storehouse was empty, and now he took it that he could have the princess.

The king went out to the storehouse, and empty it was, that was sure enough. Cinderlad was both black and sooty and the king thought it too bad that such a tramp should have his daughter. So he said he had a cellar filled with beer and old wine, three hundred barrels of each kind, which he would have him drink first. "And it is all the same, if you can drink them up by this time tomorrow, you shall have her," said the king.

"I'll have to try," said Cinderlad, "but perhaps you don't mind my taking one of my companions along with me?"

"Yes, gladly," said the king, for he thought there was so much beer and wine, they would soon be out of the play, all seven of them.

Cinderlad then called the one who was sucking the bung and always was so thirsty for beer, and the king locked them up in the cellar. There he drank barrel after barrel as long as there was any left, but in the last barrel he left enough for a couple of mugs for each of his comrades.

In the morning the cellar was unlocked, and Cinderlad went at once to the king and said he had finished the beer and the wine, and now he took it that he could have the princess as the king had promised.

"Yes, but first I must go down to the cellar and see," said the king, for he couldn't believe it. But when he got there, he found nothing but empty barrels. Now Cinderlad was both black and sooty, and the king thought it wouldn't do at all to have such a son-in-law. So he said it was all the same, if Cinderlad could get water from the end of the world in ten minutes for the princess's tea he should have both her and half the kingdom; for that was certainly quite impossible, he thought.

"I'll have to try," said Cinderlad.

Then he got hold of the one who was jumping about on one leg and had seven ship's pound weights tied to the other. And said he had better untie the weights and use both legs as fast as he could, for in less than ten minutes he must have water from the end of the world for the princess's tea. The man untied the weights, got a bucket and set off, and right away he was out of sight. But they waited and they waited and he didn't come back, and at last there was but three minutes left of the time and the king was as pleased as if he had won half a dollar.

But then Cinderlad called the one who could hear the grass growing, and told him to listen and find out what had become of the other. "He has fallen asleep at the well," he said. "I can hear him snoring, and the troll is scratching his head."

Then Cinderlad called the one who could shoot to the end of the world and told him to send a bullet into the troll. Yes, so he did; he took good aim and shot it right through the eye. The troll gave such a roar that he woke the man who had come to get water for the tea, and when he reached the king's hall there was still a minute left out of the ten.

Cinderlad went straight to the king and said that here was the water, and now he took it for granted that he could have the princess, for surely there could be no more talk about that. But the king thought he was just as black and sooty now as before, and didn't like having him for son-in-law. So he said he had three hundred cords of wood in the oast house with which he was going to dry his grain. "And it is all the same," he said, "if you are able to sit in there and burn it all up, you shall have her. There shan't be any more talk about that."

The Ship That Went As Well by Land As by Sea

"I'll have to try," said Cinderlad, "but perhaps you don't mind my taking one of my companions along?"

"Yes, even all the six of them," said the king, for he thought it would be hot enough for all of them.

Cinderlad called the one who had the seven summers and the fifteen winters in his body, and went over to the oast house in the evening. But the king had put plenty of wood on the fire, you may be sure, the heat was so strong and the flame so high they could well have melted iron in the room. Out again they couldn't get, for they had hardly got in before the king had locked the door behind them and put a couple of padlocks on it besides.

So Cinderlad said: "You'll have to let out some six or seven winters, then we'll have nice summer weather here." Then the heat was just so that they could bear it. But during the night it became a little too cool, so Cinderlad said he had better heat up a little with a couple of summers, and then they slept till far into the next day.

But when they heard the king shuffling around outside, Cinderlad said: "Now you'll have to let out a couple of more winters, but mind that you handle it so that the last one flies straight into the king's face." Yes, he did so, and when the king opened the door to the oast house, expecting to find them all burnt to cinders, they were sitting there huddling and shivering so their teeth rattled. And the one with the fifteen winters in his body let the last one out right into the king's face, so it swelled up in a big chilblain.

"Can I have the princess now?" said Cinderlad.

"Yes, take her and keep her and take the kingdom into the bargain," said the king. He didn't dare to say no any longer.

So the wedding took place, and they feasted and made noise and shot off fire crackers and guns.

All the while they were running about looking for gun wads, so they caught me to use me for one, gave me some porridge in a bottle and some milk in a basket, and then they shot me all the way here so I could tell how it all happened.

The Quern That Stands and Grinds at the Bottom of the Sea

A LONG, long time ago there were two brothers, one rich and one poor. Now, one Christmas Eve, the poor one hadn't so much as a crumb in the house, either of meat or of bread, so he went to his brother to ask him for something to keep Christmas with, in God's name. It was not the first time his brother had been forced to help him, to be sure, but stingy he had always been and he wasn't very glad to see his face this time either. But he said:

"If you will do what I ask you to do, I'll give you a whole cured ham."

The poor brother said he would do anything, and was full of thanks in the bargain.

"Here is the ham; now go straight to Hell," said the rich one, and threw the ham at him.

"Well, what I have given my word to do, I must stick to," said the other; so he took the ham and set off. He walked and he walked the whole day long, and at dusk he came to a place where he saw a very bright light.

"Maybe this is the place," said the man with the ham, to himself. In the courtyard there was a wood-shed, and there stood an old man with a long white beard, hewing wood for the Christmas fire.

"Good even," said the man with the ham.

"The same to you; whither are you going so late?" said the man.

"Oh, I'm going to Hell, if I am on the right road," answered the poor man.

"Yes, you've taken the right road, for Hell is here," said the old man. "When you get inside, they will be all for buying your ham, for pork is

The Quern That Stands and Grinds

rare food in Hell; but mind you don't sell it, unless you get the hand-quern which stands behind the door for it. When you come out, I'll teach you how to handle the quern, for it's good to grind almost anything."

Well, the man with the ham thanked the other for his good advice, and knocked at the Devil's door.

When he got in, everything went just as the old man had said. All the devils, great and small, came swarming up to him like ants round a snake, and each tried to outbid the other for the ham.

"Well," said the man, "by rights my wife and I ought to have this ham for our Christmas dinner; but since you have all set your hearts on it, I suppose I must give it up to you. But if I sell it at all, I'll have for it that quern behind the door yonder."

At first the Devil wouldn't hear of such a bargain, and chaffered and haggled with the man; but he stuck to what he said, and at last the Devil had to part with his quern. When the man got out into the yard, he asked the old woodcutter how to use it. And when he had learned how to set the quern right, he thanked the old man and went off home as fast as he could. But still the clock had struck twelve on Christmas Eve before he reached his own door.

"Wherever in the world have you been?" said his wife. "Here have I sat hour after hour waiting and watching, without so much as two sticks to lay together under the Christmas porridge."

"Oh," said the man, "I couldn't get back before, for I had quite something to run for and a long way I had to go too. But now you shall see."

So he put the quern on the table and bade it first of all grind lights, then a table-cloth, then meat, then ale, and so on till they had got everything that was nice for Christmas fare. And the quern ground out what he wished, just as soon as he spoke the word. The wife stood by, blessing her stars, and kept on asking where he had got hold of this quern, but he wouldn't tell her.

"It's all one where I got it from. You see the quern is a good one, and the mill-stream never freezes," said the man.

33

The Quern That Stands and Grinds

So he ground meat and drink and dainties enough to last out till Twelfth Day, and on the third day he asked all his friends and kin to his house, and gave a great feast. Now, when his rich brother saw all that was on the table, and all that was behind in the larder, he grew quite spiteful and wild, for he begrudged his brother everything.

" 'Twas only on Christmas Eve," he said to the rest, "he was in such straits that he came and asked for a morsel of food in God's name, and now he gives a feast as if he were count or king." And he turned to his brother and said:

"But where, in the name of Hell, did you get all this wealth?" he asked his brother.

"From behind the door," answered the owner of the quern, for he didn't care to let the cat out of the bag. But later in the evening, when he had got a drop too much, he could keep his secret no longer, and brought out the quern and said:

"There you see what has gotten me all this wealth." And so he made the quern grind all kinds of things. When his brother saw it, he set his heart on having the quern, and at long last he was to have it. But he had to pay three hundred dollars for it, and his brother bargained to keep it till hay-harvest came, "for if I keep it that long, I shall have ground up food enough to last me for many years," he thought. During that time you may be sure the quern didn't stand idle long enough to get rusty, and when hay-harvest time came, the rich brother got it. But the other took care not to teach him how to handle it.

It was evening when the rich brother got the quern home, and next morning he told his wife to go out into the hay-field and toss, while the mowers cut the grass, and he would stay at home and get the dinner ready. So, when dinner time drew near, he put the quern on the kitchen table.

"Grind herrings and broth, and grind them good and fast," said the man.

So the quern began to grind herrings and broth; first of all, all the dishes full, then all the tubs full, and so on till the kitchen floor was quite

34

covered. Then the man twisted and twirled at the quern to get it to stop, but for all his twisting and fingering the quern went on grinding. And in a little while the broth rose so high that the man was like to drown. So he threw open the kitchen door and ran into the parlour, but it wasn't long before the quern had ground the parlour full too. And it was only at the risk of his life that the man could get hold of the latch of the house door through the stream of broth. When he got the door open, he ran out and set off down the road, with the stream of herrings and broth at his heels, roaring like a waterfall over the whole farm.

Now the wife, who was in the field tossing hay, thought it a long time to dinner, and at last she said:

"Well, though the master doesn't call us home, we may as well go. Maybe he finds it hard work to boil the broth and will be glad of my help."

The men were willing enough, so they sauntered homeward. But just as they had got a little way up the hill, what should they meet but herrings and broth and bread, all running and dashing and splashing together in a stream, and the master himself running before them for his life. And as he passed them, he bawled out:

"Would to heaven each of you had a hundred throats! But take care you're not drowned in the broth."

Away he went, as though the Evil One were at his heels, to his brother's house, and begged him for God's sake to take back the quern that instant; for, said he:

"If it grinds only one hour more, the whole parish will be swallowed up by herrings and broth."

But his brother wouldn't hear of taking it back till the other paid him down three hundred dollars more.

So the poor brother got both the money and the quern, and it wasn't long before he set up a farm house far finer than the one in which his brother lived. And with the quern he ground so much gold that he covered the house with plates of the purest gold; and as the farm lay by the seaside, one could see it gleam and glisten far off at sea. All who sailed

The Quern That Stands and Grinds

by put ashore to see the rich man in the golden house, and to see the wonderful quern, the fame of which spread far and wide till there was hardly anybody who hadn't heard tell of it.

A long while later there came a skipper who wanted to see the quern, and the first thing he asked was if it could grind salt.

"Grind salt!" said the owner. "I should just think it could. It can grind anything."

When the skipper heard that, he said he must have the quern, cost what it would; for if only he had it, he thought he should be rid of his long voyages across stormy seas for a lading of salt. Well, at first the man wouldn't hear of parting with the quern, but the skipper begged and prayed so hard that at last he let him have it. But he had to pay many, many thousand dollars for it. Now, when the skipper had got the quern on his back, he made off with it at once, for he was afraid lest the man should change his mind; so he had no time to ask how to handle the quern, but got on board his ship as fast as he could, and set sail. When he sailed a good way off, he brought the quern on deck.

"Grind salt, and grind both good and fast," said the skipper.

Well, the quern began to grind salt so that it poured out like water. When the skipper had got the ship full, he wished to stop the quern, but whichever way he turned it, and however much he tried, it was no good— the quern kept grinding on. And the heap of salt grew higher and higher, and at last down sank the ship.

There lies the quern at the bottom of the sea, and grinds away at this very day, and that's why the sea is salt.

The Maid
on the Glass Mountain

ONCE upon a time there was a man who had an outlying field high up in the hills somewhere, and in the field there was a barn which he had built to keep his hay in. But there had not been much in the barn for the last year or two, I should say, for every Midsummer Night, when the grass stood greenest and deepest, the meadow was eaten down to the very ground, just as if a whole drove of cattle had been browsing there overnight. This happened once, and it happened twice. But then the man grew weary of losing his crop of hay, and said to his sons—he had three of them, and the youngest one was Cinderlad, of course—that now one of them must go and sleep in the barn on the outlying field during Midsummer Night, for it was too much that his grass should be eaten root and blade this year, as it had been the last two years. So whichever of them went must keep a sharp look-out, said the man.

Well, the eldest son wanted to go and watch the meadow, trust him for looking after the grass so well that neither man nor beast nor the Devil himself would get a blade of grass! So when evening came, he set off to the barn and lay down to sleep. But a little on in the night there came such a clatter and such an earthquake that walls and roof shook, and up jumped the lad and took to his heels as fast as ever he could, nor dared he once look round. And the grass was all eaten up this year, as it had been twice before.

Next Midsummer Night the man said again it would never do to lose all the grass in the outlying field year after year. Now one of the sons must go and watch it, and watch it well too. Well, the next eldest son

38

wanted to try his luck that night. So he went over to the barn and lay down to sleep, just as his brother had done. But as the night wore on, there came a rumbling and quaking of the earth, still worse than the last Midsummer Night. And when the lad heard this he got frightened, and took to his heels as fast as if he were paid for it.

Next year the turn came to Cinderlad, but when he made ready to go, the other two began to laugh and make fun of him.

"Yes, you are just the one to watch the hay," they said. "You who have done nothing all your life but sit in the ashes and toast yourself by the fire."

But Cinderlad didn't care a pin for what they said. As evening drew on, he strolled over to the outlying field. There he went inside the barn and lay down; but after a while the barn began to roar and rumble so that it was dreadful to hear.

"Oh, if it doesn't get worse, I think I can stand it," thought Cinderlad. to himself.

A little while after came another roar and an earthquake, so hay and straw flew about the lad's ears.

"Oh, if it doesn't get worse, I think I can stand it," thought the lad.

But just then came the third rumbling, and an earthquake, so the lad thought that walls and roof were coming down on his head. But when that was over, all of a sudden it was still as death about him.

"I wonder if it will come again," thought Cinderlad. But no, it didn't come again. Still it was and still it stayed. But when he had lain for a little while, he heard a noise as if a horse stood chewing just outside the barn door. He stole to the door and peeped through a chink to see what it was, and there stood a horse feeding away. So big and fat and grand a horse Cinderlad had never set eyes on, and saddle and bridle were on it, and a full set of armour for a knight, and all was of copper, so bright that the light gleamed from it.

"Ho-ho," thought the lad, "so it is you that eat up our hay. I'll soon put a spoke in your wheel. Just see if I don't."

He hurried and pulled the fire-steel out of his pocket, and threw it over the horse. Then it had no power to stir from the spot, and became so tame that the lad could do what he liked with it. So he got on the horse and rode off to a place which no one knew of. There he put up the horse.

When he got home, his brothers laughed and asked how he had fared.

"You didn't lie long in the barn, even if you had the heart to go so far as the field," they said.

"Well, I lay in the barn till the sun rose, and neither saw nor heard anything," said Cinderlad. "I can't think what it was in the barn that made you both so afraid."

"Oh, we shall soon see how well you have watched the field," said the brothers. But when they arrived at the field, there stood the grass just as deep and thick as it had been the evening before.

Next Midsummer Night it was the same story over again; neither of the elder brothers dared to go out to the outlying field to watch the crop; but Cinderlad, he had the heart to go; and everything happened just as it had happened the year before. First there was a clatter and an earthquake, and after a while another, and then still another. But all three earthquakes were much, much worse this year. Then all at once everything was still as death, and the lad heard something cropping the grass outside the barn door. He stole to the door as quiet as could be and peeped through a chink. Well, there, right against the wall, stood another horse, chewing and champing with might and main. It was far finer and fatter than the one that came the year before, and it had a saddle on its back and a bridle and bit and full suit of mail for a knight— all of shiny silver and as grand as you would wish to see.

"Ho-ho, it is you that gobble up our hay tonight," thought the lad. "I'll soon put a spoke in your wheel." And with that he took his fire-steel out of his pocket and threw it over the horse's crest, and there it stood as tame as a lamb. Well, the lad rode this horse, too, to the hiding place where he kept the other one, and after that he went home.

"How pretty the outlying field must look today!" said the brothers.

"Well, so it does," said Cinderlad.

Off ran the others to see, and there stood the grass thick and deep as the day before, but they didn't give Cinderlad softer words for all that.

Now when the third Midsummer Night came, the two elder still hadn't the heart to lie out in the barn and watch the grass, for they had got so scared at heart the night they lay there before that they couldn't get over the fright. But Cinderlad, he dared to go. And the very same thing happened now as had happened twice before. Three earthquakes came, one after the other, each worse than the one which went before; and when the last came, the lad danced about with the shock from one barn wall to the other. And after that, all at once it was still as death.

Now when he had lain a little while, he heard something tugging away at the grass outside the barn, so he stole again to the door chink and peeped out, and there stood a horse close outside—far, far bigger and fatter than the two he had taken before.

"Ho-ho, it is you that come to eat up our hay this time," thought the lad. "I'll soon stop that—I'll soon put a spoke in your wheel." He pulled his fire-steel out of his pocket and threw it over the horse's neck, and in a trice it stood as if it were nailed to the ground, and Cinderlad could do as he pleased with it. Then he rode off with it to the hiding place where he kept the other two, and then he went home again.

There his two brothers made fun of him, as they had done before, saying they could see he had watched the grass well, for he looked for all the world as if he were walking in his sleep. But Cinderlad gave no heed to them; he asked them only to go and see for themselves. And when they went—there stood the grass as fine and deep as it had been twice before.

The king of the country where Espen Cinderlad's father lived had a daughter, whom he would give only to the man who could ride up the Mountain of Glass, for close by the king's farms there was a high mountain all of glass, as smooth and slippery as ice.

Upon the tiptop of the mountain, the king's daughter was to sit with three golden apples in her lap, and the one who could ride up and snatch the three golden apples was to have her and half the kingdom. This the king had stuck up on all the church doors in his realm, and in many other kingdoms besides. The princess was so beautiful that everyone who saw her fell over head and ears in love with her, whether he would or no, so you may be sure that all the princes and knights were eager to win her —and half the kingdom besides.

They came riding from all parts of the world on high prancing horses, clad in the grandest attire; for there wasn't one of them who hadn't made up his mind that he, and he alone, was to win the princess.

So when the day came which the king had fixed, there was such a crowd of princes and knights under the glass mountain that it made one's head whirl to look at them. And everyone in the country who could even crawl along was bound for the place to see who would win the king's daughter; and the two elder brothers set off with the rest. But as for Cinderlad, they said outright he shouldn't go with them, for if they were seen with such a changeling, all begrimed with smut from sitting in the fireplace poking the ashes, they said folk would make game of them.

"Well," said Espen Cinderlad, "it's all one to me. I can go alone and stand or fall by myself."

Now when the two brothers came to the glass mountain, the knights and princes were all hard at it, riding their horses till they were all in foam. But it was no good, by my troth, for as soon as ever the horses set foot on the mountain, down they slipped, and there wasn't one who could get a yard or two up. And no wonder, for the mountain was as slippery as a windowpane and as steep as a house wall. But all were eager to have the princess and half the kingdom, so they rode and slipped and slipped and rode, and still it was the same story over again. At last all their horses were so weary that they could scarce lift a leg, and in such a sweat that the lather dripped from them, and so the knights had to give up. The king was just thinking that he would proclaim that the riding was to start over again the next day, to see if they might have better luck, but just then a knight came riding up on a horse so grand that no one had ever seen the like of it in all his born days, and the knight had mail of copper, and the horse a copper bit in his mouth, so bright that the sunbeams shone from it. The others called out to him he might just as well spare himself the trouble of trying to ride up the glass mountain, for it

would lead to no good, but he gave no heed to them. He put his horse at the mountain, and went up it like nothing for a good way, about a third of the height or so; and when he had got so far, he turned his horse round and rode down again. So handsome a knight the princess thought she had never yet seen; and while he was riding, she sat and thought to herself: "Would to heaven he might only come up!"

And when she saw him turning his horse, she threw down one of her golden apples after him, and it rolled down into his shoe. But when he came down from the mountain, he rode off at such a speed that no one could tell what had become of him. That evening all the princes and knights were to pass before the king, that he who had ridden so far up the mountain might show the golden apple which the princess had thrown. But there was no one who had anything to show. One after another they all came, but not a man of them could show the apple.

In the evening the brothers of Espen Cinderlad came home, and had such a long story to tell about the riding up the glass mountain.

"At first," they said, "there was not one of the whole lot who was able to get as much as a stride up, but then there came one who had a suit of copper mail and a copper bridle and saddle too, all so bright that you could see them shining and gleaming far away," they said. "That was a chap who knew how to ride. He rode a third of the way up the Mountain of Glass, and he could easily have ridden the whole way up, if he chose; but he turned round and rode down, thinking, maybe, that was enough for once."

"Oh, I should so like to have seen him, that I should," said Cinderlad, who sat in the fireplace poking the ashes as was his wont.

"Oh," said the brothers, "you would, would you? You look fit to keep company with squires and lords, you slovenly thing, sitting there amongst the ashes."

Next day the brothers were to set off again, and Espen Cinderlad asked them this time, too, to let him go with them and see the riding. But no, they wouldn't have him at any price; he was too loathsome and ugly, they said.

The Maid on the Glass Mountain

"Well, well," said Cinderlad, "it is all one to me. I can go alone and stand or fall by myself."

So when the brothers got to the Mountain of Glass, all the princes and knights began to ride again. And you may be sure they had taken care to shoe their horses sharp, but it was no good. They rode and slipped and slipped and rode, just as they had done the day before, and there was no one who could get so far as a yard up the glass mountain. And when they had worn out their horses so they could not stir a leg, they were forced to give up again. The king was just thinking that he might as well proclaim that the riding should take place the day after for the last time, to see if perhaps they might have better luck; but then it came across his mind that he might as well wait a little longer to see if the knight in copper mail would come this day too. Well, he saw nothing of him. But all at once there came one riding on a horse far, far grander than that on which the knight in copper had ridden; and this knight had silver mail and a silver saddle and bridle, all so bright that the sunshine gleamed and glanced from them far away. The others shouted to him again, saying he might as well save himself the trouble of trying to ride up the Mountain of Glass. But the knight paid no heed to them; he rode straight at the mountain and right up it till he had gone two thirds of the way, then he wheeled his horse round and rode down again. Him the princess liked still better than the knight in copper, and she sat and wished he might only be able to come right up to the top. But when she saw him turning back, she threw the second apple after him, and it rolled right down into his shoe. But as soon as ever he had come down from the Mountain of Glass, he rode off so fast that no one could see what became of him.

In the evening, when all were to pass before the king and his daughter, so that he who had the golden apple might show it, in they went, one after the other, but there was no one who had any apple to show. And the two brothers, as they had done on the day before, went home and told how things had gone; how all had ridden and none had got up.

"But at long last," they said, "came one in a silver suit, and his horse had a silver saddle and a silver bridle. He was just a chap to ride; and he got two thirds up the Mountain of Glass and then turned back. What a boy! And to him the princess threw the second golden apple," said the brothers.

"Oh," said Espen Cinderlad, "I should have liked so to have seen him too, that I should."

"Well, well, he was slightly brighter than the ashes that you are poking, you ugly, dirty thing," said the brothers.

The third day everything happened as it had happened the two days before. Espen Cinderlad begged to go and see the sight, but the two wouldn't hear of his going with them. When they got to the glass mountain, there was no one who could get so much as a yard up it; and now all waited for the knight in silver mail, but they neither saw nor heard of him. At last came one riding on a horse so grand that no one had ever seen his match; and the knight had a suit of golden mail, and a golden saddle and bridle, so bright and shining that the sunbeams gleamed from them far away.

The other knights and princes were so amazed to see how grand he was that they weren't even able to get their mouths open to call out to him not to try his luck. He rode right at the glass mountain, and whirled right up as light as a feather in a gust of wind. And he tore up it so fast that the princess hadn't even time to wish that he might get up the whole way, before he was there. He snatched the third golden apple from the princess's lap, and then turned his horse and rode down again. As soon as he got down, he rode off at full speed and was out of sight in no time.

Now, when the brothers came home at night they told over and over again how the riding had gone off that day, and at last they had a deal to say about the knight in the golden mail.

"He just was a chap to ride!" they said. "So grand a knight isn't to be found in the wide world."

"Oh," said Espen Cinderlad, "I should have liked so to have seen him."

"Well, the heap of embers that you are poking is not quite so bright and gleaming, ugly, black beast that you are," said the brothers.

Next day all the knights and princes were to pass before the king and the princess—it was too late to do so the night before, I suppose—that he who had the gold apple might bring it forth. But one came after the other, first the princes and then the knights, and still no one could show the golden apple.

"Well," said the king, "someone must have it, for we all saw with our own eyes how a man came and rode up and carried it off."

So he commanded that everyone who was in the kingdom should come up to his court and see if he could show the golden apple. Well, they all came, one after another, but no one had the golden apple. And after a long time the two brothers of Espen Cinderlad also came. They were the last of all, so the king asked them if there was anyone else in his kingdom who hadn't come.

"Oh, yes," said they, "we have a brother, but he never carried off the golden apple. He hasn't stirred out of the ashes on the hearth on any of the three days."

"Never mind that," said the king. "As all the others have been in my palace, he may as well come too."

So Cinderlad had to go up to the palace.

"Have you got the golden apple? Speak out," said the king.

"Yes, here is the first and here is the second and here is the third one too," said Espen Cinderlad, and with that he pulled all three golden apples out of his pocket, and at the same time threw off his sooty rags and stood before them in his gleaming golden mail.

"Yes," said the king, "you shall have my daughter and half my kingdom, for you well deserve both her and it."

So they got ready for the wedding, and Espen Cinderlad got the king's daughter for wife. There was great merry-making at the bridal feast, you may fancy; for they could all be merry, though they couldn't ride up the Mountain of Glass. And if they haven't stopped their feasting yet, why, they are still at it.

The Widow's Son

ONCE on a time there was a poor, poor widow, who had an only son. She dragged on with the boy till he had been confirmed, and then she said she couldn't feed him any longer, he must just go out and earn his own bread. So the lad wandered out into the world, and when he had walked a day or so, a strange man met him.

"Where are you going?" asked the man.

"Oh, I'm going out into the world to try and get a place," said the lad.

"Will you come and serve me?" said the man.

"Oh, yes, just as soon as anyone else," said the lad.

"Well, you'll have a good place with me," said the man, "for you'll only have to keep me company, and do nothing at all else beside."

So the lad stopped with him and lived on the fat of the land, both in meat and drink, and had little or nothing to do; but he never saw a living soul in that man's house.

So one day the man said:

"Now I'm going off for eight days, and that time you'll have to spend here all alone; but you must not go into anyone of these four rooms. If you do, I'll take your life when I come back."

"No," said the lad, he'd be sure not to do that. But when the man had been gone three or four days, the lad couldn't bear it any longer, but went into the first room, and when he got inside he looked round, but he saw nothing but a shelf over the door where a bramble-bush rod lay.

Well, thought the lad, a pretty thing to forbid my seeing this.

So when the eight days were out, the man came home, and the first thing he said was:

"You haven't been into any of these rooms, of course."

"No, no, that I haven't," said the lad.

"I'll soon see that," said the man, and went at once into the room where the lad had been.

"Nay, but you have been in here," said he, "and now you shall lose your life."

Then the lad begged and prayed so hard that he got off with his life, but the man gave him a good thrashing. When it was over, they were as good friends as ever.

Some time after the man set off again, and said he should be away fourteen days; but before he went he forbade the lad to go into any of the rooms he had not been in before; as for that he had been in, he might go into that, and welcome. Well, it was the same story over again, except that the lad stood out eight days before he went in. In this room, too, he saw nothing but a shelf over the door, and a big rubble-stone and a pitcher of water on it. Well, after all, there's not much to be afraid of my seeing here, thought the lad.

But when the man came back, he asked if he had been into any of the rooms. No, the lad hadn't done anything of the kind.

"Well, well, I'll soon see that," said the man, and when he saw that the lad had been in them after all, he said:

"Ah, now I'll spare you no longer! Now you must lose your life."

But the lad begged and prayed for himself again, and so this time too he got off with stripes, though he got as many as his skin could bear. But when he got sound and well again, he led just as easy a life as ever, and he and the man were just as good friends.

So a while after the man was to take another journey, and now he said he should be away three weeks, and he forbade the lad anew to go into the third room, for if he went in there he might just make up his mind at once to lose his life. Then after fourteen days the lad couldn't bear it, he slipped into the room, but he saw nothing at all in there but a trap-door on the floor. And when he lifted it up and looked down, there stood a great copper cauldron which bubbled and boiled away down there; but he saw no fire under it.

The Widow's Son

"Well, I should just like to know if it's hot," thought the lad, and stuck his finger down into the broth, and when he pulled it out again, lo! it was gilded all over. The lad scraped and scrubbed it, but the gilding wouldn't go off, so he bound a piece of rag round it, and when the man came back and asked what was the matter with his finger, the lad said he'd given it such a bad cut. But the man tore off the rag, and then he soon saw what was the matter with the finger. First he wanted to kill the lad outright, but when the lad wept and begged, he only gave him such a thrashing that he had to keep his bed three days. After that the man took down a pot from the wall and rubbed him over with some stuff out of it, and so the lad was sound and fresh as ever.

After a while the man started off again, and this time he was to be away a month. But before he went, he said to the lad, if he went into the fourth room, he might give up all hope of saving his life.

Well, the lad stood out for two or three weeks, but then he couldn't hold out any longer; he must and would go into that room, and so in he stole. There stood a great black horse tied up in a stall by himself, with a manger of red-hot coals at his head, and a truss of hay at his tail. The lad thought this all wrong, so he changed them about, and put the hay at his head. Then said the horse:

"Since you are so good at heart as to let me have some food, I'll set you free, that I will. For if the troll comes back and finds you here, he'll kill you outright. But now you must go up to the room which lies just over this, and take a coat of mail out of those that hang there; and mind, whatever you do, don't take any of the bright ones, but the rustiest of all you see, that's the one to take; and sword and saddle you must choose for yourself just in the same way."

So the lad did all that; but it was a heavy load for him to carry them all down at once.

When he came back, the horse told him to pull off his clothes and get into the cauldron which stood and boiled in the other room, and bathe himself there. "If I do," thought the lad, "I shall look an awful fright"; but for all that, he did as he was told. When he had taken his bath, he became so handsome and sleek, and as red and white as milk and blood, and much stronger than he had been before.

"Do you feel any change?" asked the horse.

"Yes," said the lad.

"Try to lift me, then," said the horse.

Oh, yes, he could do that; and as for the sword, he brandished it like a feather.

"Now saddle me," said the horse, "and put on the coat of mail, and then take the bramble-bush rod and the rubble-stone and the pitcher of water and the pot of ointment, and then we'll be off as fast as we can."

When the lad had got on the horse, off they went at such a rate he couldn't at all tell how they went. But when he had ridden awhile, the horse said:

"I think I hear a noise. Look around! Can you see anything?"

"Yes, there are ever so many coming after us, at least a score," said the lad.

"Yes, that's the troll," said the horse. "Now he's after us with his pack."

So they rode on awhile, until those who followed were close behind them.

"Now throw your bramble-bush rod behind you, over your shoulder," said the horse; "but mind you throw it a good way off my back."

So the lad did that, and all at once a close, thick bramble-wood grew up behind them.

Then the lad rode on a long, long time, while the troll and his crew had to go home to fetch something to hew their way through the wood. But after a while the horse said again:

"Look behind you! Can you see anything now?"

"Yes, ever so many," said the lad, "as many as would fill a large church."

"Yes, that's the troll and his crew," said the horse. "Now he's got more to back him; now throw down the rubble-stone, and mind you throw it far behind me."

And as soon as the lad did what the horse said, up rose a great big rubble-stone mountain behind him. So the troll had to be off home to fetch something to mine his way through the rock; and while the troll did that, the lad rode a good bit further on. Then the horse asked him to look behind him, and then he saw a troop like a whole army behind him, and their armour glistened in the sunbeams.

"Yes," said the horse, "that's the troll. Now he's got his whole band with him; now throw the pitcher of water behind you, but mind you don't spill any of it upon me."

The lad did that; but in spite of all the pains he took, he spilled one drop on the horse's flank. Then it became a great deep lake; and because of that one drop, the horse found himself far out in it, but still he swam safe to land. When the trolls came to the lake, they lay down to drink it all up and they lapped and sopped it and gobbled it down till they burst.

"Now we're rid of them," said the horse.

Then they travelled a long, long while, and at last they came to a green patch in a wood.

"Now strip off all your arms," said the horse, "and only put on your ragged clothes; and take the saddle off me and let me loose; and hang my gear and your arms up inside that great hollow lime-tree yonder. Then make yourself a wig of fir-moss, and go up to the king's palace, which lies close here, and ask for a place. Whenever you need me, only come here and shake the bridle, and I'll come to you."

Yes, the lad did all his horse told him, and as soon as ever he put on the wig of moss he became so ugly, and pale, and miserable to look at, no one would have known him. Then he went up to the king's palace and begged first for leave to be in the kitchen and bring in wood and water for the cook, but then the kitchen-maid asked him:

"Why do you wear that ugly wig? Off with it. I won't have such a fright in here."

"No, I can't do that," said the lad. "My head isn't quite clean."

"Do you think I'll have you in here about the food when you are as dirty as that?" cried the cook. "Away with you to the coachman; you're best fit to go and clean the stable."

But when the coachman told him to take his wig off, he got the same answer, and he wouldn't have him either.

"You'd best go down to the gardener," said he; "you're best fit to go about and dig in the soil."

There he got leave to stay, but none of the other servants would sleep with him, and so he had to sleep by himself under the steps of the summerhouse. It stood upon beams and had a high staircase. Under that he got some moss for a bed, and there he lay as well as he could.

When he had been some time at the palace, it happened one morning just as the sun rose, that the lad had taken off his wig and stood and washed himself, and then he was so handsome it was a joy to look at him.

The king's daughter saw from her window the lovely gardener's boy, and thought she had never seen anyone so handsome. So she asked the gardener why his boy lay out there under the steps.

"Oh," said the gardener, "none of his fellow-servants want to share bed with him; that's why."

"Let him come up tonight and lie beside the door in my room, so the other servants won't think themselves too good to share room with him any longer," said the princess.

The gardener told that to the lad.

"Do you think I'll do any such thing?" said the lad. "Then they'd start to gossip about the princess and me."

"Yes," said the gardener, "you've good reason to fear any such thing, you who are so handsome, you."

"Well," said the lad, "since it's your will, I suppose I must go."

When he was to go up the steps in the evening, he tramped and stamped so on the way, that they had to beg him to tread softly lest the king should come to know it. He came into the princess's room, lay down, and began to snore at once.

"Steal over and take off his wig," said the princess to her maid.

But just as she was going to whisk it off, he caught hold of it with both hands, and said she should never have it. After that he lay down again and began to snore. Then the princess gave her maid a wink, and this time she whisked off the wig, and there lay the lad so lovely and white and red, just as the princess had seen him in the morning sun.

After that the lad slept every night in the princess's room.

But it wasn't long before the king came to hear how the gardener's boy had slept every night in the princess's room, and he got so wroth he almost took the lad's life. He didn't do that, however, but threw him into the prison tower; and as for his daughter, he shut her up in her own room, whence she never got leave to stir day or night. All that she begged and all that she prayed, for the lad and herself, was no good. The king was only more wroth than ever.

Some time after came a war, and the king had to take up arms against another king who wished to take his kingdom from him. When the lad heard that, he begged the jailer to go to the king and ask for a coat of mail and a horse, and for leave to go to the war. All the rest laughed when the jailer told his errand, and begged the king to let him have an old worn-out suit, that they might have the fun of seeing such a wretch in battle. He got that, and an old broken-down nag besides, which went upon three legs and dragged the fourth after it.

Then they went out to meet the foe, but they hadn't got far from the palace before the lad got stuck fast in a bog with his nag. There he sat, nodding and stuttering. "Hey, will you up? Hey, will you up?" he said to the nag. And all the rest had their fun out of this, and laughed and made game of the lad as they rode past him. But they were scarcely gone, before he ran to the lime-tree, threw on his coat of mail, and shook the bridle, and there came the horse in a trice, and said:

"Do now your best, and I'll do mine."

When the lad came up the battle was raging, and the king was in a sad pinch; but no sooner had the lad rushed into the thick of it than the foe was beaten back and put to flight. The king and his men wondered and wondered who it could be who had come to help them, but none of them got so near him as to be able to talk to him, and as soon as the battle was over he was gone. When they went back, there sat the lad still in the bog, nodding and pulling at his three-legged nag, and they all laughed again.

"No, only just look!" they said. "There the fool sits still."

The next day when they went out to battle, they saw the lad sitting there still, so they laughed again and made game of him; but as soon as ever they had ridden by, the lad ran again to the lime-tree, and all happened as on the first day. Everyone wondered what strange champion it could be that had helped them, but no one got so near him as to say a word to him; and no one guessed it could be the lad, that's easy to understand.

When they rode homewards at night, and saw the lad still sitting there on his nag, they burst out laughing at him again, and one of them shot an arrow at him and hit him in the leg. So he began to shriek and to bewail. 'Twas enough to break one's heart; and so the king threw his pocket-handkerchief to him to bind his wound.

When they went out to battle the third day, the lad still sat there.

"Hey, will you up? Hey, will you up?" he said to his nag.

"Nay, nay," said the king's men, "if he won't stick there till he's starved to death."

And then they rode on, and laughed at him till they were fit to fall from their horses. When they were gone, he ran again to the lime, and came up to the battle just in the very nick of time. This day he slew the enemy's king, and then the war was over at once.

When the battle was over, the king caught sight of his handkerchief, which the strange warrior had bound round his leg, and so it wasn't hard to find him out. They took him with great joy among them to the palace, and the princess, who saw him from her window, got so glad no one can believe it.

"Here comes my sweetheart true," she said.

Then he took the pot of ointment and rubbed himself on the leg, and after that he rubbed all the wounded, and so they all got well again in a moment.

56

The Widow's Son

Thus he got the princess for bride; but when he went down into the stable, where his horse was, on the day the wedding was to be, there it stood so dull and heavy, and hung its ears down, and wouldn't eat its corn. As the young king—for he was now a king and had got half the kingdom—spoke to him and asked what ailed him, the horse said:

"Now I have helped you on, and now I won't live any longer. So just take the sword, and cut my head off."

"No, I'll do nothing of the kind," said the young king; "but you shall have all you want, and rest all your life."

"Well," said the horse, "if you don't do as I tell you, see if I don't take your life somehow."

So the king had to do what he asked; but when he swung the sword and was to cut the head off, he was so sorry he turned away his face, for he would not see the stroke fall. But as soon as ever he had cut off the head, there stood the loveliest prince on the spot where the horse had stood.

"Why, where in all the world did you come from?" asked the king.

"It was I who was a horse," said the prince, "for I was king of that land whose king you slew yesterday. He it was who threw this troll's shape over me, and sold me to the troll. But now he is slain I get my own again, and you and I will be neighbour kings, but war we will never make on one another."

And they didn't either, for they were friends as long as they lived and each paid the other very many visits.

Lord Per

ONCE on a time there was a poor couple. They had nothing in the world but three sons. What names the two elder had I can't say, but the youngest, he was called Per. When their father and mother died, the sons were to share what was left, but there was nothing but a porridge-pot, a griddle, and a cat.

The eldest, who was to have first choice, he took the pot, "for," said he, "whenever I lend the pot to anyone to boil porridge, I can always get leave to scrape it."

The second took the griddle, "for," said he, "whenever I lend it to anyone, I'll always get a morsel of dough to make a bite to taste."

But the youngest, he had no choice left him. If he was to choose anything, it must be the cat.

"Well," said he, "if I lend the cat to anyone I shan't get much by that; for if pussy gets a drop of milk, she'll want it all herself. Still, I'd best take her along with me. I shouldn't like her to go about here and starve."

So the brothers went out into the world to try their luck, and each took his own way. But when the youngest had gone awhile, the cat said:

"Now you shall have a good turn, because you wouldn't let me stay behind in the old cottage and starve. Now I'm off to the wood to lay hold of a fine fat head of game, and then you must go up to the king's house that you see over there, and say you are come with a little present for the king. And when he asks who sends it, you must say that it is from Lord Per."

Well, Per hadn't waited long before the cat came back with a reindeer from the wood. She had jumped up on the reindeer's head, between

58

his horns, and said: "If you don't go straight to the king's house I'll claw your eyes out."

So the reindeer had to go whether he liked it or no.

And when Per got to the palace, he went into the kitchen with the deer and said: "Here I'm come with a little present for the king, if he won't despise it."

The king came out into the kitchen, and when he saw the fine plump reindeer he was very glad.

"But, my dear friend," he said, "who in the world is it that sends me such a fine gift?"

"Oh, it comes from Lord Per!" said the boy.

"Lord Per! Lord Per!" said the king. "Let me see, now, where is it that he lives?" for he thought it a shame not to know so great a man. But that was just what the lad wouldn't tell him. He daren't do it, he said, because his master had forbidden him.

So the king gave him a good gift of money, and bade him be sure and say all kinds of pretty things, and many thanks for the present to his master when he got home.

Next day the cat went again into the wood and jumped up on the head of a stag and sat between his horns, and forced him to go to the palace. Then Per went again into the kitchen, and said he was come with a little present for the king, if he would be pleased to take it. And the king was still more glad to get the stag than he had been to get the reindeer, and asked again who it was that sent so grand a gift.

"Why, it's Lord Per," said the lad; but when the king wanted to know where Lord Per lived, he got the same answer as the day before. And this day he gave Per a still bigger lump of money.

The third day the cat came with an elk. And so when Per got into the king's kitchen and said he had a little present for the king, if he'd be pleased to take it, the king came out at once into the kitchen. And when he saw the grand big elk, he was so glad he scarce knew which leg to stand on. And this day he gave Per still more money; it must have been a hundred dollars. He wished now, once for all, to know where this Lord Per lived, and asked and asked about this thing and that, but the lad said he daren't say, for the sake of his master, who had strictly forbidden him to tell.

"Well, then," said the king, "beg Lord Per to come and see me."

Yes, the lad would take that message; but when Per got out into the yard again and met the cat, he said:

"A pretty scrape you've got me into now, for here's the king, who wants me to come and see him, and you know I've nothing to go in but these rags I stand and walk in."

"Oh, don't you worry about that," said the cat. "In three days you shall have coach and horses, and fine clothes, so fine that the gold falls from them, and then you may go and see the king very well. But mind, whatever you see in the king's palace, you must say you have far finer and grander things of your own. Don't forget that."

No, no, Per would bear that in mind, never fear.

So when three days were over, the cat came with a coach and horses, and clothes, and all that Per wanted; and altogether it was as grand as anything you ever set eyes on. Then he set off and the cat ran alongside the coach. The king met him well and graciously; but whatever the king offered him and whatever the king showed him, Per said 'twas all very well, but he had far finer and better things in his own house. The king did not like this any too well, but Per stuck to what he said. And at last the king got so angry, he couldn't bear it any longer.

"Now I'll go home with you," he said, "and see if it be true what you've been telling me, that you have far finer and better things of your own. But if you've been telling a pack of lies, heaven help you."

"Now, you've got me into a fine scrape," said Per to the cat, "for here's the king coming home with me; but my home—that's not so easy to find, I think."

"Oh, never mind!" said the cat. "Only do you drive after me as I run before."

So off they set; first Per, who drove after his cat, and then the king and all his court.

When they had driven a good bit, they came to a great flock of fine sheep that had wool so long it almost touched the ground.

"If you'll say," said the cat to the shepherd, " 'This flock of sheep belongs to Lord Per,' when the king asks you, I'll give you this silver spoon"—which she had taken with her from the king's palace.

Yes, he was willing enough to do that. So when the king came up, he said to the lad who watched the sheep:

"Well, I never saw so large and fine a flock of sheep in my life! Whose is it, my little lad?"

"Why," said the lad, "whose should it be but Lord Per's?"

A little while after they came to a great, great herd of fine brindled cows, who were all so sleek the sun shone from them.

"If you'll say," said the cat to the shepherd girl, " 'This herd is Lord Per's,' when the king asks you, I'll give you this silver ladle." And the ladle, too, she had taken from the king's palace.

"Yes, with all my heart!" said the shepherd girl.

When the king came up, he was quite amazed at the fine fat herd, for such a herd he had never seen before, and so he asked the girl who owned the cows she was herding.

"Why, who should own them but Lord Per!" said the girl.

So they went on a little further and came to a great, great drove of horses, the finest you ever saw—great and fat, and six of each shade, red and dun and blue.

"If you'll say this drove of horses is Lord Per's when the king asks you," said the cat, "I'll give you this silver bucket." And the bucket, too, she had taken from the palace.

Yes, the lad was willing enough. And so when the king came up, he was quite amazed at the grand drove of horses, for the matches of such horses he had never yet set eyes on, he said.

He asked the lad who watched them whose all the red and dun and blue horses were.

"Whose should they be," said the lad, "but Lord Per's?"

When they had gone a good bit farther, they came to a castle. First there was a gate of brass, and next there was a gate of silver, and next a gate of gold. The castle itself was of silver, and glistened so bright that it hurt the eyes, for the sun shone full upon it as they arrived.

There they entered, and the cat told Per to say this was his house. As for the castle inside, it was far finer than it looked outside, for everything was pure gold—chairs, and tables, and benches, and all. And when the king had gone all over it and seen everything high and low, he got quite shameful and downcast.

"Yes," he said at last, "Lord Per has everything far finer than I have, there's no gainsaying that." And so he wanted to be off home again.

But Per begged him to stay to supper, and the king stayed, but he was sour and surly the whole time.

While they sat at supper, back came the troll who owned the castle, and knocked at the gate.

"Who's this eating my meat and drinking my mead like swine in here!" roared the troll.

As soon as the cat heard that, she ran down to the gate.

"Stop a bit and I'll tell you how the farmer sets to work to get in his winter rye," said the cat.

"First of all, you see, he ploughs his field, and then he dungs it, and then he ploughs it again, and then he harrows it." And so she went on till the sun rose.

"Oh, do look behind you, and there you'll see such a lovely lady," said the cat to the troll.

So the troll turned around and, of course, as soon as he saw the sun he burst.

"Now all this is yours," said the cat to Lord Per. "Now you must cut off my head; that's all I ask for what I have done for you."

"Nay, nay," said Lord Per. "I'll never do any such thing, that's flat."

"If you don't," said the cat, "see if I don't claw your eyes out."

Well, so Lord Per had to do it, though it was sore against his will. He cut off the cat's head, but there and then she became the loveliest princess you ever set eyes on, and Lord Per fell in love with her at once.

Lord Per

"Yes, all this greatness was mine first!" said the princess. "But a troll bewitched me to be a cat in your father's and mother's cottage. Now you may do as you please, whether you take me as your queen or not, for you are now king over all this realm."

Well, well, there was little doubt Lord Per would be willing enough to have her as his queen, and so there was a wedding-feast that lasted eight whole days. And after it was over, I stayed no longer with Lord Per and his queen.

Soria Moria Castle

THERE once was a couple who had a son and his name was Halvor. Ever since he was a little boy he had never wanted to do a thing, but just sat there and poked in the cinders. His parents often put him out to learn this trade or that, but Halvor could stay nowhere; for, when he had been there a day or two, he ran away from his master, and never stopped till he was sitting again in the fireplace poking about in the cinders.

But then one day a skipper came, and asked Halvor if he hadn't a mind to be with him, and go to sea, and see strange lands. Yes, Halvor would like that very much; and then he was ready at once.

I don't know how long they sailed, but after a long, long while they fell into a great storm, and when it was blown over and it got still again, they couldn't tell where they were; for they had been driven away to a strange coast that none of them knew.

As there was no wind at all, they stayed lying wind-bound there, and Halvor asked the skipper leave to go on shore and look about. He would sooner go, he said, than lie there and sleep.

"Do you think now you're fit to show yourself before folk?" said the skipper. "Why, you've no clothes but those rags you stand in."

But Halvor kept on asking and so at last he got leave, but he was to be sure and come back as soon as ever it began to blow. So off he went and found a lovely land. Wherever he went there were great plains with cornfields and meadows, but he couldn't catch a glimpse of a living soul. Then it began to blow, but Halvor thought he hadn't seen enough yet, and he wanted to walk a little farther just to see if he couldn't meet any people. After a while he came to a broad highway, so smooth and even you might easily roll an egg along it. Halvor followed this, and when evening drew on he saw a great castle far off, with lights shining from all its windows. As he had now walked the whole day and hadn't taken much to eat with him, he was very hungry, but still the nearer he came to the castle, the more afraid he got.

In the castle kitchen a great fire was blazing, and Halvor went into it; but such a kitchen he had never seen in all his born days, it was so grand and fine. There were vessels of silver and vessels of gold, but still never a living soul. When Halvor had stood there awhile and no one came out, he went and opened a door, and there inside sat a princess who spun upon a spinning wheel.

"No, oh, no!" she called out. "Dare Christian folk come hither? But you'd better leave at once or the troll will gobble you up; for here lives a troll with three heads."

"All one to me," said the lad. "I'd be just as glad to hear he had four heads besides. I'd like to see that fellow. And I won't leave, for I've done no harm; but you must get me some food, for I'm almost starved to death."

When Halvor had eaten his fill, the princess told him to try if he could brandish the sword that hung against the wall. No, he couldn't brandish it; he couldn't even lift it up.

"Well," said the princess, "then you have to take a swallow from the bottle that hangs by its side; that's what the troll does when he goes out to use the sword."

Halvor took a swallow, and in the twinkling of an eye he could brandish the sword like nothing. And now he thought it high time the troll came; and lo, just then up came the troll puffing and blowing. Halvor jumped behind the door.

"Huttetu, what a smell of Christian man's blood!" said the troll, and put his heads in through the door.

"You'll soon know that to your cost," said Halvor, and with that he hewed off all his heads.

Now the princess was so glad that she was free, she both danced and sang, but then she called her sisters to mind, and so she said:

"Would my sisters were free too!"

"Where are they?" asked Halvor.

Well, then she told him all about it: one was taken away by a troll to his castle which lay fifty miles off, and the other by another troll to his castle which was a hundred miles further still.

"But now," she said, "you must first help me to get this ugly carcass out of the house."

Yes, Halvor was so strong he swept everything away, and made it all clean and tidy in a switch. Then he had a huge meal, and next morning he set off at peep of grey dawn. He could take no rest by the way, but ran and walked the whole day. When he first saw the castle, he got a little afraid. It was far grander than the first, but here too there wasn't a living soul to be seen. So Halvor went into the kitchen, and didn't stop there either, but went further on into the house.

"No, oh, no!" called out the princess. "Dare Christian folk come hither? I don't know, I'm sure, how long it is since I came here, but in all that time I haven't seen a Christian man. 'Twere best you saw how to get away as fast as you came, for here lives a troll who has six heads."

"I shan't go," said Halvor, "if he has six heads besides."

"He'll take you up and swallow you down alive," said the princess.

But it was no good, Halvor wouldn't go; he wasn't at all afraid of the troll. But food and drink he must have, for he was half starved after his long journey. Well, he got as much of that as he wished, but then the princess wanted him to be off again.

"No," said Halvor, "I won't go. I've done no harm and I've nothing to be afraid of."

"He won't stay to ask that," said the princess, "for he'll take you without law or leave. But as you won't go, try if you can brandish that sword yonder, which the troll wields in war."

He couldn't brandish it, and then the princess said he must take a

swallow of the bottle which hung by its side, and when he had done that he could brandish it.

Just then back came the troll, and he was both stout and big, so that he had to go sideways to get through the door. When the troll got his first head in, he called out:

"Huttetu, what a smell of Christian man's blood!"

But that very moment Halvor hewed off his first head, and then all the others. The princess was so happy she didn't know on which foot to stand, but then she came to think of her sister, and wished out loud she were free too. Halvor thought that might be done, and wanted to be off at once. But first he had to help the princess to get the troll's carcass out of the way, and then the next morning he set off.

It was a long way to the castle, and he had to walk fast and run hard to reach it in time; but about nightfall he saw the castle, which was far finer and grander than either of the others. This time he wasn't the least afraid, but walked straight through the kitchen and into the castle. There sat a princess who was so pretty there was no end to her loveliness. She too, like the others, told him there hadn't been Christian folk there ever since she came thither, and bade him go away again, else the troll would swallow him alive.

"He has nine heads," she said.

"Aye, aye," said Halvor, "if he had nine other heads, and nine other heads still, I won't go away," and so he stood fast before the stove. The princess kept on begging him so prettily to go away lest the troll should gobble him up, but Halvor said: "Let him come as soon as he likes."

So she gave him the troll's sword and bade him take a swallow of the bottle, that he might be able to brandish and wield it.

Just then back came the troll puffing and blowing and tearing along. He was far stouter and bigger than the other two, and he too had to go on one side to get through the door.

"Huttetu, what a smell of Christian man's blood!" he said.

At once Halvor hewed off the first head and then all the rest. But the last was the toughest of them all, and it was the hardest bit of work

Halvor had ever done, to get that hewn off, although he knew he should be strong enough to do it.

Now all the princesses came together to that castle, and they were glad and happy as they had never been in all their lives before, and they all were fond of Halvor and Halvor was fond of them, and he might choose the one he liked best for his bride. But of the three the youngest was fondest of him.

But there after a while, Halvor went about, and was so strange and dull and silent. Then the princesses asked him what he lacked, and if he didn't like to live with them any longer. Yes, he did, for they had enough and to spare, and he was well off in every way, but still somehow or other he did so long to go home, for his father and mother were alive, and them he had such a great wish to see.

Well, they thought that might be done.

"You shall go thither and come back hither, safe and unscathed, if you will only follow our advice," said the princesses.

Yes, he'd be sure to mind all they said. So they dressed him up till he was as grand as a king's son, and then they set a ring on his finger. And that was such a ring, he could wish himself thither and hither with it. But they told him to be sure not to take it off, and not to name their names, for there would be an end of all his bravery and then he'd never see them more.

"I wish I were at home and that home were here," said Halvor, and it was done as he had wished. Before he knew a thing he found himself standing at his father's cottage door. Now it was about dusk at even, and so, when they saw such a grand stately lord walk in, the old couple got so afraid they began to bow and scrape. Then Halvor asked if he couldn't stay there, and have a lodging there that night. No, that he couldn't.

"We can't do it at all," they said, "for we haven't this thing or that thing which such a lord is used to have. 'Twere best your lordship went up to the farm, no long way off, for you can see the chimneys, and there they have lots of everything."

Halvor wouldn't hear of it—he wanted to stop. But the old couple stuck to their own, that he had better go to the farmer's; there he would get both meat and drink; as for them, they hadn't even a chair to offer him to sit down on.

"No," said Halvor, "I won't go up there till tomorrow early, but let me just stay here tonight. Worst come to the worst, I can sit in the chimney-corner."

Well, they couldn't say anything against that; so Halvor sat down by the fireplace and began to poke about in the ashes, just as he used to do when he lay at home in old days, and stretched his lazy bones.

They chattered and talked about many things; and they told Halvor about this thing and that; and then he asked them if they had never had any children.

Yes, yes, they had once a lad whose name was Halvor, but they didn't know whither he had wandered. They couldn't even tell whether he was dead or alive.

"Couldn't it be me, now?" said Halvor.

"To be sure," said the woman and moved on her chair. "Our Halvor was so lazy and idle, he never did a thing; and he was so ragged that one tatter took hold of the next tatter on him. No, there never was the making of such a fine fellow in him as you are, master."

A little while after the woman went to the hearth to poke up the fire, and when the blaze fell on Halvor's face, just as when he was at home of old poking about in the ashes, she knew him at once.

"It really is you, Halvor!" she said, and then there was such joy for the old couple there was no end to it. And he had to tell them how he had fared, and the old woman was so fond and proud of him nothing would do but he must go up at once to the farmer's, so she could show him to the lassies who had always looked down on him. And off she went first, and Halvor followed after. So, when she got up there, she told them that Halvor had come home again, and now they should only see how grand he was. "He looks just like a king's son," she said.

"All very fine," said the lassies, and tossed up their heads. "We'll be bound he's just the same beggarly ragged boy he always was."

Just then in walked Halvor, and then the lassies were all so taken aback, they forgot their shirts in the fireplace, where they were sitting dressing themselves, and ran out in their smocks. Well, when they were got back again, they were so shamefaced they scarce dared look at Halvor, towards whom they had always been proud and haughty.

"Aye, aye," said Halvor, "you always thought yourselves so pretty and neat, no one could come near you; but now you should just see the eldest princess I have set free; against her you look just like milkmaids. And the midmost is prettier still; but the youngest, who is my sweetheart, she's fairer than both sun and moon. Would to heaven they were only here," said Halvor, "then you'd see what you would see."

He had scarce uttered these words before there they stood, but then he felt so sorry, for now he remembered what they had said. Up at the farm there was a great feast got ready for the princesses, and much was made of them, but they wouldn't stop there.

"No, we want to go down to your father and mother," they said to Halvor, "and so we'll go out now and look about us."

He went with them, and they came to a great lake just outside the farm. Close by the water was such a lovely green bank; here the princesses said they would sit and rest awhile; they thought it so sweet to sit down and look over the water.

So they sat down there, and when they had sat awhile, the youngest princess said:

"I may as well scratch your head a little, Halvor."

Yes, Halvor laid his head on her lap, she scratched his head, and it wasn't long before Halvor fell fast asleep. Then she took the ring from his finger, and put another in its stead, and so she said:

"Take hold of me as I take hold of you, and would we were all in Soria Moria Castle."

When Halvor woke up, he could very well tell that he had lost the princesses, and began to weep and wail; and he was so sad, they couldn't comfort him at all. In spite of all his father and mother said, he wouldn't stop there, but took farewell of them, and said he was sure not to see them again; for if he couldn't find the princesses again, he thought it not worth while to live.

Well, he had still three hundred dollars left, so he put them into his pocket and set out on his way. So when he had walked awhile, he met a man with a tidy horse, and he wanted to buy it, and began to chaffer with the man.

"Aye," said the man, "to tell the truth, I never thought of selling him; but if we could strike a bargain, perhaps——"

"What do you want for him?" asked Halvor.

"I didn't give much for him, nor is he worth much. He's a brave horse to ride, but he can't draw at all; still he's strong enough to carry your knapsack and you too, if you walk some of the way," said the man.

At last they agreed on the price, and Halvor laid the knapsack on him, and then he walked a bit, and rode a bit, turn and turn about. At night he came to a green meadow where stood a great tree, at the roots of which he sat down. There he let the horse loose, but he didn't lie down to sleep; he opened his knapsack and took a meal. At peep of day off he set again, for he could take no rest. So he rode and walked and walked and rode the whole day through the wide wood, where there were many green spots and glades that shone so bright and lovely between the trees. He didn't know at all where he was or whither he was going, but he gave himself no more time to rest than when his horse cropped a bit of grass, and he took a snack out of his knapsack when they came to one of those green glades. So he went on walking and riding by turns, and as for the wood there seemed to be no end to it.

But at dusk the next day he saw a light gleaming away through the trees.

"Would there were folk hereaway," thought Halvor, "that I might warm myself a bit and get a morsel to eat."

When he got up to it, he saw the light came from a wretched little hut, and through the window he saw an old, old couple inside. They were as grey-headed as a pair of doves, and the old wife had such a nose! Why, it was so long that she used it for a poker to stir the fire as she sat in the fireplace.

"Good evening," said Halvor.

"Good evening," said the old wife.

"But what errand can you have in coming hither?" she went on. "For no Christian folk have been here these hundred years and more."

Well, Halvor told her all about himself, and how he wanted to get to Soria Moria Castle, and asked if she knew the way thither.

"No," said the old wife, "that I don't; but see now, here comes the Moon. I'll ask her, she'll know all about it, for doesn't she shine on everything?"

So when the Moon stood clear and bright over the tree-tops, the old wife went out.

"Thou Moon, thou Moon," she cried, "canst thou tell me the way to Soria Moria Castle?"

"No," said the Moon, "that I can't, for the time I shone there a cloud stood before me."

"Wait a bit still," said the old wife to Halvor. "By and by comes the West Wind; he's sure to know it, for he puffs and blows round every corner.

"Nay, nay," said the old wife when she went out again, "you don't mean to say you've got a horse too? Just turn the poor beastie loose in our pasture and don't let him stand starving here at the door." Then she ran on: "But won't you trade him away to me? We've got an old pair of boots here, with which you can take twenty miles at each stride. Those you shall have for your horse, and so you'll get all the sooner to Soria Moria Castle."

That Halvor was willing to do at once; and the old wife was so glad at having the horse, she was ready to dance and skip for joy.

"For now," she said, "I shall be able to ride to church. I, too—think of that."

As for Halvor, he had no rest and wanted to be off at once, but the old wife said there was no hurry.

"Lie down on the bench with you and sleep a bit, for we've no bed to offer you, and I'll watch and wake you when the West Wind comes."

So after a while up came the West Wind, roaring and howling along till the walls creaked and groaned.

Out ran the old wife.

"Thou West Wind, thou West Wind! Canst thou tell me the way to Soria Moria Castle? Here's one who wants to get thither."

"Yes, I know it very well," said the West Wind, "and now I'm just off thither to dry clothes for the wedding that's to be. If he's swift of foot he can go along with me."

Out ran Halvor.

"You'll have to stretch your legs if you mean to keep up," said the West Wind.

So off they set over hills and mountains and slopes and banks, and Halvor had hard work to keep up.

"Well," said the West Wind, "now I've no time to stay with you any longer, for I've got to go away yonder and tear down a strip of spruce wood first before I go to the bleaching-ground to dry the clothes; but if you follow this ridge you'll come to some lassies standing washing clothes, and then you've not far to go to Soria Moria Castle."

In a little while Halvor came upon the lassies who stood washing, and they asked if he had seen anything of the West Wind who was to come and dry the clothes for the wedding.

"Yes, that I have," said Halvor. "He's only gone to tear down a strip of spruce wood. It'll not be long before he's here," and then he asked them the way to Soria Moria Castle.

So they put him into the right way, and when he got to the castle, the courtyard was full of folk and horses, so full it made one giddy to look at them. But Halvor was so ragged and torn from having followed the West Wind through bush and brier that he kept aside all by himself and wouldn't go forth till the last day when the bridal feast was to be.

Soria Moria Castle

So when all were to drink the bride's and bridegroom's health and wish them luck, as was then right and fitting, and when the cupbearer was to drink to them all again, both knights and squires, last of all he came in turn to Halvor. He drank their health but let the ring that the princess had put upon his finger as he lay by the lake, fall into the cup, and bade the cupbearer go and greet the bride and hand her the cup.

Then up rose the princess from the table at once.

"Who is most worthy to have one of us," she said, "he that has set us free, or he that here sits by me as bridegroom?"

Well, they all said there could be but one voice and will as to that, and when Halvor heard that, he wasn't long in throwing off his beggar's rags and arraying himself as bridegroom.

"Yes, here is the right one after all," said the youngest princess as soon as she saw him, and so she jilted the other, and married Halvor.

Per, Paal,
and Espen Cinderlad

ONCE on a time there was a man who had three sons, Per, Paal, and Espen Cinderlad. But besides these three sons the man had nothing, for he hadn't one penny to rub against another. And so he told his sons over and over again they must go out into the world and try to earn their bread, for there at home there was nothing to be looked for but starving to death.

Now, a bit off the man's cottage was the king's farm, and just again the king's windows a great oak had sprung up, which was so stout and big that it took away all the light from the king's house. The king had said he would give many, many dollars to the man who could fell the oak, but no one was man enough for that, for as soon as ever one chip of the oak's trunk flew off, two grew in its stead. The king also wanted to have a well dug that would hold water all through the year; for all his neighbours had wells, but he hadn't any, and that he thought a shame. So the king said he would give anyone who could dig him such a well as would hold water the whole year through, both money and goods; but no one could do it, for the king's farm lay high, high up on a hill, and they hadn't dug a few inches before they came upon the living rock.

But as the king had set his heart on having these two things done, he had it given out far and wide, in all the churches of his kingdom, that he who could fell the big oak in the king's courtyard, and get him a well that would hold water the whole year round, should have the princess and half the kingdom. Well, you may easily know there was many

78

a man who came to try his luck! But for all their hacking and hewing, and all their digging and delving, it was no good. The oak got bigger and stouter at every stroke, and the rock didn't get softer either. So one day the three brothers thought they'd set off and try too, and their father hadn't a word against it; for even if they didn't win the princess and half the kingdom they might get a place somewhere with a good master, and that was all he wanted. So when the brothers said they thought of going to the king's court, their father said yes at once. So Per and Paal and Espen Cinderlad went off.

They hadn't gone far before they came to a fir wood, and up along one side of it rose a steep hillside, and then they heard something hewing and hacking away up on the hill.

"I wonder now what it is that is hewing away up yonder," said Espen Cinderlad.

"You're always so clever with your wonderings, you," said Per and Paal. "What wonder is it, pray, that a woodcutter should stand and hack up on a hillside?"

"Still, I'd like to see what it is, after all," said Cinderlad, and up he went.

"Oh, if you're such a child, 'twill do you good to learn to walk too," bawled out his brothers after him.

But Espen didn't care for what they said. He climbed the steep hillside towards where the noise came, and when he came there, he saw that it was an ax that stood hacking and hewing, all of itself, at the trunk of a fir.

"Good day!" said Espen Cinderlad. "So you stand here all alone and hew?"

"Yes, here I've stood and hewed and hacked a long, long time, waiting for you," said the ax.

"Well, here I am at last," said Espen, as he took the ax, pulled it off its haft, and stuffed both head and haft into his knapsack.

So when he got down again to his brothers, they began to jeer and laugh at him.

Per, Paal, and Espen Cinderlad

"And now, what funny thing was it you saw up yonder on the hillside?" they said.

"Oh, it was only an ax we heard," said Espen.

When they had gone a bit farther, they came under a steep spur of rock, and up there they heard something digging and shovelling.

"I wonder now," said Espen, "what it is digging and shovelling up yonder at the top of the rock."

"You're always so clever with your wonderings, you," said Per and Paal again, "as if you'd never heard a woodpecker hacking and pecking at a hollow tree."

"Well, well, but I think it would be a piece of fun just to see what it is anyway," said Espen.

And so off he set to climb the rock, while the others laughed and made game of him. But he didn't care a bit for that—up he climbed, and when he got near the top, it was a spade that stood there digging and delving.

"Good day!" said Espen Cinderlad. "So you stand here all alone, and dig and delve!"

"Yes, that's what I do," said the spade, "and that's what I've done this many a long day, waiting for you."

"Well, here I am," said Cinderlad again, as he took the spade and knocked it off its handle, and put it into his knapsack, and then went down again to his brothers.

"Well, what was it so rare and strange that you saw up there at the top of the rock?" said Per and Paal.

"Oh, it wasn't so very much. It was only a spade we heard," said Espen.

So they went on again a good bit, till they came to a brook. They were thirsty, all three, after their long walk, and so they lay down beside the brook to have a drink.

"I wonder now," said Espen, "where all this water comes from."

"I wonder if you're right in your head," said Per and Paal, in one breath. "If you're not mad already, you'll go mad very soon, with your wonderings. Where the brook comes from! Have you never heard how water rises from a spring in the earth?"

"Yes! But still I should like to see where this brook comes from," said Espen.

So up alongside the brook he went, in spite of all that his brothers bawled after him. Nothing could stop him. On he went. So, as he went up and up, the brook got smaller and smaller, and at last, a little way farther on, he saw a great walnut, and out of that the water trickled.

"Good day!" said Espen again. "So you lie here, and trickle and run down all by yourself?"

"Yes, I do," said the walnut; "and here have I trickled and run this many a long day, waiting for you."

"Well, here I am," said Cinderlad, as he took up a lump of moss and plugged up the hole, that the water mightn't run out. Then he put the walnut into his knapsack and ran down to his brothers.

"Well, now," said Per and Paal, "have you found out where the water comes from? A rare sight it must have been!"

"Oh, after all, it was only a hole it ran out of," said Espen; and so the others laughed and made game of him again, but Espen Cinderlad didn't mind that a bit.

"After all, I had the fun of seeing it," said he.

When they had gone a bit farther, they came to the king's farm. But as everyone in the kingdom had heard how they might win the princess and half the realm, if they could only fell the big oak and dig the king's well, so many had come to try their luck that the oak was now twice as stout and big as it had been at first. For two chips grew for every one they hewed out with their axes, as I dare say you all bear in mind. So the king had now laid it down as a punishment, that if anyone tried and couldn't fell the oak, he should be put on a barren island, and both his ears were to be clipped off. But the two brothers didn't let themselves be scared by that. They were quite sure they could fell the oak, and Per, as he was eldest, was to try his hand first. But it went with him as with all the rest who had hewn at the oak; for every chip he cut out, two grew in its place. So the king's men seized him, and clipped off both his ears, and put him out on the island.

Now Paal, he was to try his luck, but he fared just the same. When he had hewn two or three strokes, they began to see the oak grow, and so the king's men seized him too, and clipped his ears, and put him out on the island. And his ears they clipped closer, because they said he ought to have taken a lesson from his brother.

Now Espen Cinderlad was to try.

"If you will look like a marked sheep, we're quite ready to clip your ears at once, and then you'll save yourself some bother," said the king, for he was angry with him for his brothers' sake.

"It would be fun to try anyway," said Espen, and so he got leave. He took his ax out of his knapsack and fitted it to its haft.

"Hew away!" said he to his ax; and away it hewed, making the chips fly again, so that it wasn't long before down came the oak.

When that was done, Espen pulled out his spade and fitted it to its handle.

"Dig away!" said he to the spade; and so the spade began to dig and delve till the earth and rock flew out in splinters, and so he had the well soon dug out, you may be sure.

And when he had got it as big and deep as he chose, Espen Cinderlad took out his walnut and laid it in one corner of the well and pulled out the plug of moss.

"Trickle and run," said Espen; and so the nut trickled and ran, till the water gushed out of the hole in a stream, and in a short time the well was brimful.

So Espen had felled the oak which shaded the king's house, and dug a well in the courtyard, and so he got the princess and half the kingdom, as the king had said. But it was lucky for Per and Paal that they had lost their ears, else they had heard each hour and day how everyone said that Espen Cinderlad hadn't done so badly with his wondering after all.

Cinderlad and the Troll

ONCE on a time there was a poor man who had three sons. When the father died, the two elder set off into the world to try their luck, but the youngest they wouldn't have with them at any price.

"As for you," they said, "you're fit for nothing but to sit and poke about in the cinders."

"Then I'll have to go alone," said Cinderlad.

So the two went off and got places at the king's farm—the one under the coachman, and the other under the gardener. Cinderlad set off too, and took with him a great kneading-trough, which was the only thing his parents had left behind them, but which the other two would not bother themselves with. It was heavy to carry, but he did not like to leave it behind, and so, after he had trudged a bit, he too came to the king's farm, and asked for a place. They told him they did not want him, but he begged so prettily that at last he got leave to be in the kitchen, and carry in wood and water for the cook. He was quick and ready, and in a little while everyone liked him; but the two others were dull, and so they got more kicks than halfpence, and grew quite envious of Cinderlad when they saw how much better he got on.

Just opposite the king's house, across a lake, lived a troll, who had seven silver ducks which swam on the lake, so that they could be seen from the king's windows. These the king had often longed for, and so the two elder brothers told the coachman:

"If our brother only chose, he has said he could easily get the king those seven silver ducks."

You may be sure it wasn't long before the coachman told this to the king. And the king called Cinderlad before him, and said:

84

Cinderlad and the Troll

"Your brothers say you can get me the silver ducks, so now go and fetch them."

"I'm sure I never thought or said anything of the kind," said the lad.

"You did say so, and you shall fetch them," said the king, who would hold his own.

"Well! well!" said the lad. "Needs must, I suppose; but give me a bushel of rye and a bushel of wheat, and I'll try what I can do."

So he got the rye and the wheat, and put them into the kneading-trough he had brought with him from home, got in, and rowed across the lake. When he reached the other side, he began to walk along the shore, and to sprinkle and strew the grain, and at last he coaxed the ducks into his kneading-trough, and rowed back as fast as ever he could.

When he got half over, the troll came out of his house and set eyes on him.

"Is it you that have gone off with my seven silver ducks?" roared the troll.

"Yes!" said the lad.

"Will you be back again?" asked the troll.

"Perhaps," said the lad.

When he got back to the king with the seven silver ducks, he was more liked than ever, and even the king was pleased to say: "Well done!" But at this his brothers grew more and more spiteful and envious, and so they went and told the coachman that their brother had said, if he chose, he was man enough to get the king the troll's bedspread, which had a gold square and a silver square, and a gold square and a silver square. And this time, too, the coachman was not slow in telling all this to the king. So the king told the lad how his brothers had said he was good to steal the troll's bedspread, with gold and silver squares. So now he must go and do it, or lose his life.

Cinderlad answered that he had never thought or said any such thing; but when he found there was no help for it, he asked for three days to think out a plan.

When the three days were gone, he rowed over in his kneading-trough again, and went spying about. At last he saw those in the mountain come out and hang the bedspread out to air, and as soon as ever they had gone back into the mountain, Cinderlad pinched it and rowed away with it as fast as he could.

When he was half across out came the troll and set eyes on him.

"Is it you who took my seven silver ducks?" roared the troll.

"Yes!" said the lad.

"And now, have you taken my bedspread, with a silver square and gold square, and a silver square and gold square?"

"Yes!" said the lad.

"Will you come back again?" said the troll.

"Perhaps," said the lad.

But when he got back with the gold and silver bedspread, everyone was fonder of him than ever, and he was made the king's body-servant.

At this, the brothers were still madder, and, to be revenged, they went and told the coachman:

"Now, our brother has said he is man enough to get the king the gold harp which the troll has, and that harp is of such a kind that all who listen when it is played grow glad, however sad they may be."

Yes, the coachman went and told the king, and he said to the lad:

"If you have said this, you shall do it. If you do it, you shall have the princess and half the kingdom. If you don't, you shall lose your life."

"I'm sure I never thought or said anything of the kind," said the lad; "but if there's no help for it, I may as well try; but I must have six days to think about it."

Yes, he might have six days; but when they were over, he must set out.

Then he took a tenpenny nail, a birch-pin, and a stump of a candle in his pocket, and rowed across, and walked up and down outside the mountain where the troll lived, looking stealthily about him. After a while the troll came out and caught sight of him.

"Is it you who took my seven silver ducks?" roared the troll.

"Yes," said the lad.

"Then it is you who took my bedspread with the gold and silver squares, too?" asked the troll.

"Yes," said the lad.

So the troll caught hold of him at once and took him off into the mountain.

"Now, my daughter," said the troll, "I've caught the fellow who stole my silver ducks and my bedspread with the gold and silver squares. Put him into the fattening coop, and when he's fat, we'll butcher him, and make a feast for our friends."

She was willing enough, and put him at once into the fattening coop, and there he stayed eight days, fed on the best, both in meat and in drink, and as much as he could cram. So, when the eight days were over, the troll said to his daughter to go down and cut him in his little finger, that they might see if he was fat. Down she came to the coop.

"Out with your little finger!" she said.

But Cinderlad stuck out his tenpenny nail, and she cut at it.

"Oh, no, he's as hard as iron still," said the troll's daughter, when she came back again to her father. "We can't take him as yet." Eight days later the same thing happened, and this time Cinderlad stuck out the birchen pin.

"He is a little better," she said, when she got back to the troll, "but still he'll be as hard as wood to chew."

But when another eight days were gone, the troll told his daughter to go down and see if he wasn't fat now.

"Out with your little finger," said the troll's daughter, when she reached the coop, and this time Cinderlad stuck out the candle-stump.

"Now he is fine," she said.

"That's fine," said the troll. "Then I'll just set off and ask the guests. Meantime you must butcher him, and then roast half and boil half."

When the troll had left, the daughter began to sharpen a great long knife.

"Is that what you're going to kill me with?" asked the lad.

Cinderlad and the Troll

"Yes it is," said she.

"But it isn't sharp," said the lad. "Just let me sharpen it for you, and then you'll find it easier work to kill me."

So she let him have the knife, and he began to rub and sharpen it on the whetstone.

"Now let me try it on one of your hair plaits," said the lad. "I think it's about right now."

He got leave to do that; but at the same time that he grasped the plait of hair, he pulled back her head, and at one stroke, cut off the troll's daughter's head. And half of her he roasted and half of her he boiled, and served it all up.

After that he dressed himself in her clothes, and sat away quietly in the corner.

So when the troll came home with his guests, he called out to his daughter—for he thought all the time it was his daughter—to come and take a snack.

"Oh, no," said the lad, "I don't care for food, I'm so sad and downcast."

"You ought to know the cure for that," said the troll. "Take the gold harp and play a tune on it."

"Yes!" said the lad. "But where has it got to? I can't find it."

"Why, you know well enough," said the troll. "You used it last. Where should it be but over the door yonder?"

The lad did not wait to be told twice. He took down the harp, and went in and out playing tunes; but all at once he shoved off the kneading-trough, jumped into it, and rowed off, so that the foam flew around the trough.

After a while the troll thought his daughter was a long while gone and went out to see what ailed her; and then he saw the lad in the trough far, far out on the lake.

"Is it you that took my seven silver ducks?" he roared.

"Yes!" said the lad.

"Then you are the one that took my bedspread with the gold and silver squares, too?"

"Yes!" said the lad.

"And now you have taken away my gold harp?" roared the troll.

"Yes, so I did," said the lad.

"And haven't I eaten you up after all, then?"

"No, no! 'Twas your own daughter you ate," answered the lad.

When the troll heard that, he was so angry he burst. And then Cinderlad rowed back, and took a whole heap of gold and silver with him, as much as the trough could carry. And when he came to the king with the gold harp, he got the king's daughter and half the kingdom, as the king had promised him. And, as for his brothers, he treated them well, for he thought they had only desired his good when they said what they had said.

The Big Bird Dam

ONCE on a time there was a king who had twelve daughters, and he was so fond of them they must always be at his side. But every day at noon, while the king slept, the princesses went out to take a walk. Once, while the king was taking his noontide nap, and the princesses had gone to take their walk, all at once they disappeared and did not return. There was great sorrow all over the land, but the most sorry of all was the king. He sent messengers throughout his own and other realms, and gave out their names in all the churches, and had the bells tolled for them in all the steeples. But gone the princesses were, and gone they stayed, and none had seen any trace of them. So it was as clear as day that a troll must have carried them off into the mountain.

It wasn't long before these tidings spread far and wide, over land and town, aye, over many lands. And the news came also to a king in a far away land, who had twelve sons. When these princes heard of the twelve king's daughters, they asked leave of their father to go out and seek them. They had hard work to get his leave, for he was afraid he would never see them again, but they all fell down on their knees before the king and begged so long, at last he was forced to let them go.

He fitted out a ship for them and gave them the Red Knight for their helmsman, for the knight knew well the ways of the sea. They sailed about a long, long time, landed on every shore they came to, and hunted and asked after the princesses; but they could neither hear nor see anything of them. There were but a few days more and they would have sailed for seven years, when one day a great storm rose, and such foul weather they thought they should never come to land again, and all had to work so hard they couldn't get a wink of sleep so long as the storm lasted. But on the third day the wind fell, and all at once it got as still as still could be. Now they were all so weary with work and the rough weather they fell fast asleep right away. But the youngest prince, he could get no rest, and couldn't go off to sleep at all.

As he was pacing up and down the deck, the ship came to a little island, and on the island ran a little dog that bayed and barked at the ship as if it wanted to come on board. The prince walked up and down the deck whistling and calling the dog, but the more he whistled and coaxed, the more the dog barked and whined. He thought it a shame the dog should run about there and starve, for he thought that it must have come thither from a ship that had been cast away in the storm; but still he thought he should never be able to help it after all, for he couldn't put out the boat by himself, and as for the others, they all slept so sound he wouldn't wake them for the sake of a dog. But the weather was so calm and still; and he said to himself: "Come what may, you must go on shore and save that dog." So he tried to launch the boat, and he found it far easier work than he had thought. He rowed ashore and went up to the dog; but every time he tried to catch it, it jumped to one side, and so it went on till he found himself inside a great grand castle, before he knew where he was. Then the dog, all at once, was changed into a lovely princess; and there, on the bench, sat a man so big and ugly the prince almost lost his wits for fear.

"You've no need to be afraid," said the man—but the prince got far more afraid when he heard his gruff voice—"for I know well enough what you want. There are twelve princes of you, and you are looking for the twelve princesses that are lost. I know, too, very well whereabouts they are. They're with my lord and master, and there they sit, each of them on a golden chair, and scratch his heads, for he has twelve heads. And now you have sailed seven years, but you'll have to sail seven years more before you find them. As for you, you might stay here and welcome, and have my daughter. But you must first slay him, for he's hard master to all of us and we're all weary of him; and when he's dead,

I shall be king in his stead. But first try if you can brandish this sword," said the troll prince.

The king's son took hold of a rusty old sword which hung on the wall, but he could scarce stir it.

"Now you must take a drink from this bottle," said the troll; and when the king's son had done that, he could stir it; and when he had taken another, he could lift it; and when he had taken a third, he could brandish the sword as easily as if it had been a rolling pin.

"Now, when you get on board," said the troll prince, "you must hide the sword well in your berth, that the Red Knight mayn't set eyes on it. He's not man enough to wield it, but he'll get spiteful against you and try to take your life. And when seven years are almost out, all but three days," he went on to say, "everything will happen just as now. Foul weather will come on you, with a great storm, and when it is over you'll all be sleepy. Then you must take the sword and row ashore, and so you'll come to a castle where all sorts of guards will stand—wolves and bears and lions; but you needn't be afraid of them, for they'll all come and crouch at your feet. But when you come inside the castle, you'll soon see the troll. He sits in a splendid chamber in grand attire and array; twelve heads he has of his own, and the princesses sit round them, each on her golden chair, and scratch his heads, and you may be sure that they don't like that work. Then you must make haste, and hew off one head after the other as quick as you can; for if he wakes and sets his eyes on you, he'll swallow you alive."

Then the king's son went on board with the sword, and he bore in mind what he had come to know. The others still lay fast asleep and snored, and he hid the sword in his berth so that neither the Red Knight nor any of the rest got sight of it. It began to blow again, and he woke up the others and said he thought they oughtn't to sleep any longer, now when there was such a good wind. And there was none of them that marked he had been away. Now after the seven years were all gone but three days, all happened as the troll had said. A great storm and foul weather came on that lasted three days, and when it had blown itself out, all the rest grew sleepy and went to rest. But the king's youngest son rowed ashore, and the guards fell at his feet, and so he came to the castle. When he got inside the chamber, there sat the huge troll fast asleep as the troll prince had said, and the twelve princesses sat each on her chair and each scratched one of his heads. The king's son beckoned to the princesses to get out of the way. They pointed to the troll, and beckoned to him again to go his way as quick as ever he could; but he kept on making signs to them to get out of the way, and then they understood that he wanted to set them free and stole away softly one after the other, and as fast as they went, he hewed off the troll king's heads, till at last the blood gushed out like a great brook. When the troll was slain, the prince rowed back to the ship and hid his sword. He had done enough, he thought, and as he couldn't get rid of the body by himself, he thought it only fair they should help him a little. So he woke them all up and said it was a shame they should be snoring there, when he had found the princesses and set them free from the troll. The others only laughed at him and said he had been just as sound asleep as they, and slept even heavier than they and dreamed that he was such a man. But the king's youngest son told them all about it, and then they followed him to the land and saw first of all the brook of blood, and then the castle and the troll and the princesses. Then they saw plain enough that he had spoken the truth, and now they helped him to throw the body and the heads into the sea. So all were glad and happy, but none more so than the princesses, who were freed from having to sit there and scratch the troll's heads all day long. Of all the silver and gold and precious things that were there, they took as much as the ship could hold, and then they went on board all together, princes and princesses alike.

But when they had gone a bit out on the sea, the princesses said they had forgotten in their joy their gold crowns; they lay behind in a chest, and they would be so glad to have them. So when none of the others was willing to fetch them, the king's youngest son said:

"I have already dared so much, I can very well go back for the gold crowns too, if you will only strike sail and wait here till I come again."

Yes, that they would do. But when he had gone back so far that they couldn't see him any longer, the Red Knight, who wanted to be their chief and to have the youngest princess, said it was no use their lying there still waiting for him, for they might know very well he would never come back. They all knew, too, how the king had given him all powers and authority to sail or not, as he chose. And now they must all say 'twas he who had saved the princesses, and if anyone said anything else, he should lose his life.

The princes didn't dare to do anything else than what the Red Knight willed, and so they sailed away.

Meanwhile the king's youngest son rowed to land, went up to the castle, found the chest with gold crowns in it, and at last lugged it down to the boat and shoved off. But when he came where he ought to have seen the ship, lo! it was gone. As he couldn't catch a glimpse of it anywhere, he could very soon tell how matters stood. To row after them was no good, and so he was forced to turn about and row back to land. He was rather afraid to stay alone in the castle all night, but there was no other house to be got, so he plucked up heart, locked up all the doors and gates fast, and lay down in a room where there was a bed ready made. But fearful and woeful he was, and still more afraid he got when he had lain awhile and something began to creak and groan and quake in wall and roof, as if the whole castle were being torn asunder. Then all at once down something plunged by the side of his bed. It sounded like a whole cartload of hay. Then all was still again; but after a while he heard a voice which bade him not to be afraid, and said:

> I am Dam, the Bird of Deed,
> I will help you to succeed.

"But the first thing you must do, when you wake in the morning, is to go to the barn and fetch four barrels of rye for me. I must fill my crop with them for breakfast, else I can't do anything."

When he woke up, sure enough there he saw an awfully big bird, which had a feather at the nape of his neck, as thick and long as a half-grown spruce-fir. So the king's son went down to the barn to fetch four barrels of rye for the Big Bird Dam, and when he had crammed them into his crop, he told the king's son to hang the chest with the golden crowns on one side of his neck, and as much gold and silver as would weigh it down on the other side, and after that to get on his back and hold fast by the feather in the nape of his neck. So away they went through the air till the wind whistled after them, and so it wasn't long before they outstripped the ship. The king's son wanted to go on board for his sword, for he was afraid lest anyone should get sight of it, since the troll had told him that mustn't be; but Bird Dam said that mustn't be either.

"The Red Knight will never see it, never fear; but if you go on board, he'll try to take your life, for he has set his heart on having the youngest princess. But make your mind quite easy about her, for she lays a naked sword by her side in bed every night."

So after a long, long time they came to the island where the troll prince was, and there the king's son was welcomed so heartily there was no end to it. The troll prince didn't know how to be good enough to him for having slain his lord and master, and so made him King of the Trolls; and he would gladly have given the king's son his daughter and half the kingdom. But the king's son had so set his heart on the youngest of the twelve princesses he could take no rest, but was all for going after their ship time after time. The troll king begged him to be quiet a little longer, and said they had still nearly seven years to sail before they got home. As for the princess, the troll said the same thing as Bird Dam had said.

"You needn't fret yourself about her, for she lays a naked sword by her side every night in bed. And now if you don't believe what I say," said the troll, "you can go on board when they sail by here, and see for yourself, and fetch the sword too, for I may just as well have it again."

So when they sailed by, another great storm arose; and when the king's son went on board, they all slept, and each princess lay beside her

prince. But the youngest lay alone with a naked sword beside her in the bed, and on the floor by the bedside lay the Red Knight. The king's son took the sword and rowed ashore again, and none of them had seen that he had been on board. But still the king's son couldn't rest, and he often and often wanted to be off, and so at last when it got near the end of the seven years, and only three weeks were left, the troll king said:

"Now you may get ready to go, since you won't stay with us; and you shall have the loan of my iron boat, that sails of itself if you only say:

" 'Boat, go on!'

"In that boat there is an iron club, and that club you must lift a little, when you see the ship straight ahead of you, and then they'll get such a rattling fair breeze they'll forget to look at you. But when you get alongside them, you must lift the club a little again, and then they'll get such a foul wind and storm, they'll have something else to do than to stare at you. And when you have run past them, you must lift the club a third time, but you must always be sure to lay it down carefully again, else there'll be such a storm both you and they will be wrecked and lost. When you have got to land, you've no need to bother yourself at all about the boat. Just turn it about, and shove it off, and say:

" 'Boat, go back home the same way you came!' "

When he set out, they gave him so much gold and silver, and so many other costly things, and clothes and linen which the troll princess had sewn and woven for him all that long time, that he was far richer than any of his brothers.

Well, he had no sooner seated himself in the boat, and said: "Boat, go on!" than away went the boat. And when he saw the ship right ahead, he lifted up the club, and then they got such a fair breeze they forgot to look at him. When he was alongside the ship, he lifted the club again, and then such a storm arose and such foul weather, that the white foam flew about the ship, and the billows rolled over the deck, and they had something else to do than to stare at him. And when he had run past them, he lifted the club the third time, and then the storm and the wind rose so they had still less time to look after him, and to make him out. So he came to land long, long before the ship; and when he had got all his goods out of the boat, he shoved it off again and turned it about, and said:

"Boat, go back home the same way you came!"

Then he dressed himself as a sailor and went up to a wretched hut where an old woman lived, whom he got to believe that he was a poor sailor who had been on board a great ship that was wrecked, and that he was the only soul that had got ashore. After that he begged for house-room for himself and the goods he had saved.

"Heaven mend me!" said the old woman. "How can I lend anyone house-room? Look at me and mine—I've no bed to sleep on myself, still less one for anyone else to lie on."

Well, well, it was all the same, said the sailor; if only he got a roof over his head, it didn't matter where he lay. So she couldn't turn him out of the house, when he was so thankful for what there was. In the evening he fetched up his things, and the old woman, who was very eager to hear a bit of news to run about and tell, began at once to ask who he was, whence he came, where he had been, whither he was bound, what it was he had with him, what his business was, and if he hadn't heard anything of the twelve princesses who had vanished many, many years ago. All this she asked and much more, which it would be waste of time to tell. But he said he was so poorly and had such a bad head-ache after the awful weather he had been out in that he couldn't answer any of her questions; she must just leave him alone and let him rest a few days till he came to himself after the hard work he'd had in the gale, and then she'd know all she wanted and more than that.

The very next day the old woman began to stir him up and ask again, but the sailor's head was still so bad he hadn't got his wits together. But somehow he let drop a word or two to show that he did know something about the princesses. Off ran the old woman with what she had heard to all the gossips and chatterboxes round about, and soon the one came running after the other to ask about the princesses—if he had seen them, if they would soon be there, if they were on the way, and much more

of the same sort. He still went on groaning over his headache after the storm, so that he couldn't tell them all about it. But this much he told them—unless the princesses had been lost in the great storm, they'd make the land in about a fortnight or before perhaps; but he couldn't say for sure whether they were alive or no; for though he had seen them, it might very well be that they had been cast away in the storm since. So what did one of these old gossips do but run up to the palace with this story, and say that there was a sailor down in such and such an old woman's hut, who had seen the princesses, and that they were coming home in a fortnight or in a week's time. When the king heard that, he sent a messenger down to the sailor to come up to him and tell the news himself.

"I don't see how it's to be," said the sailor, "for I haven't any clothes fit to stand in before the king."

But the king said he must come; for the king must and would talk with him, whether he were richly or poorly clad, for there was no one else who could bring him any tidings of the princesses. So he went up at last to the palace and went in before the king, who asked him if it were true that he had seen anything of the princesses.

"Yes, I have," said the sailor. "I've seen them sure enough, but I don't know whether they're still alive, for when I last saw them, the weather was so foul we in our ship were cast away; but if they're still alive they'll be here in a fortnight or perhaps before."

When the king heard that, he was almost beside himself for joy; and when the time came that the sailor had said they would come, the king drove down to the strand to meet them in great state; and there was joy and gladness over the whole land when the ship came sailing in with the princes and princesses and the Red Knight. But no one was gladder than the old king, who had got his daughters back again. The eleven eldest princesses, too, were glad and merry; but the youngest, who was to have the Red Knight, wept and was always sorrowful. The king took this ill, and asked why she wasn't cheerful and merry like the others. She hadn't anything to be sorry for now when she had got out of the troll's clutches, and was to have such a husband as the Red Knight. She dared not say anything, for the Red Knight had said he would take the life of anyone who told the truth how things had gone.

But now one day, when they were hard at work sewing and stitching the bridal array, in came a man in a great sailor's cloak with a pedlar's pack on his back, and asked if the princesses wouldn't buy something fine of him for the wedding—he had so many wares and costly things, both gold and silver. Yes, they might do that perhaps, so they looked at his wares and they looked at him, for they thought they had seen both him and many of his costly things before.

"He who has so many fine things," said the youngest princess, "must surely have something still more precious, and which suits us better even than these."

"Maybe I have," said the pedlar.

But now all the others cried hush, and bade her bear in mind what the Red Knight had said he would do.

Some time after, the princesses sat and looked out of the window, and then the king's son came again with the great sea-cloak thrown about him, and the chest with the gold crowns at his back; and when he got into the palace hall, he unlocked the chest before the princesses, and when each of them knew her own gold crown again, the youngest said:

"I think it only right that he who set us free should get the reward that is his due; and he is not the Red Knight, but this man who has brought us our gold crowns. He it is that set us free."

Then the king's son cast off the sailor's cloak, and stood there far finer and grander than all the rest. And so the old king made them put the Red Knight to death. And now there was real downright joy in the palace. Each prince took his princess for bride and then there was a wedding-feast which was heard of and talked about throughout twelve realms.

Kari Woodenskirt

ONCE on a time there was a king who had become a widower. By his queen he had a daughter, who was so gentle and lovely there wasn't a sweeter princess in all the world. The king went on a long time sorrowing for the queen, whom he had loved so much, but at last he got weary of living alone and married another queen, who was a widow and had an only daughter too. But this daughter was just as mean and ugly as the other was kind and pretty. The stepmother and her daughter were jealous of the king's daughter because she was so lovely; but as long as the king was at home, they dared not do her any harm, he was so fond of her.

After a time he fell into war with another king and went out to battle with his host, and then the stepmother thought she might do as she pleased. And so she both starved and beat the king's daughter, and was after her in every hole and corner of the house. At last she thought everything too good for her, and turned her out to herd cattle. So there the princess went about with the cattle, and herded them in the woods and on the mountains. As for food, she got little or none; and she grew thin and wan, and was always sobbing and sorrowful. Now in the herd there was a great blue bull, which always kept himself so neat and sleek, and often he came up to the princess and let her pat him. So one day when she sat there, sad and sobbing and sorrowful, he came up to her and asked her outright why she was always in such grief. She answered nothing, but went on weeping.

"Ah," said the bull, "I know all about it quite well, though you won't tell me. You weep because the queen is bad to you, and because she is trying to starve you to death. But food you've no need to fret about, for

103

in my left ear lies a cloth; and when you take and spread it out, it will serve you with as many dishes as you please."

So she did that—took the cloth and spread it out on the grass, and lo! it served up the nicest dishes one could wish to have. There were wine, and meat, and sweet cake, too. Now, she soon regained her health again, and grew so plump and rosy and white that the queen and her scrawny chip of a daughter turned blue and yellow for spite. The queen couldn't at all make out how her stepdaughter got to look so well on such bad fare, so she told one of her maids to go after her in the wood and watch and see how it all was, for she thought some of the servants in the house must give her food. The maid went after her and watched in the wood, and there she saw how the stepdaughter took the cloth out of the bull's ear and spread it out, and how it served up the nicest dishes, which the stepdaughter ate and made good cheer over. So the maid went home and told this to the queen.

And now the king came home from war, and had won the fight against the other king with whom he went out to battle. So there was great joy throughout the palace, and no one was gladder than the king's daughter. But the queen shammed sick, and took to her bed, and paid the doctor a great fee to get him to say she could never be well again unless she had some of the blue bull's meat to eat. Both the king's daughter and the servants asked the doctor if nothing else would help her, and prayed hard for the bull, for everyone was fond of him, and they all said there wasn't that bull's match in all the land. But no, he must and should be slaughtered, nothing else would do. When the king's daughter heard that, she got very sad, and went down into the byre to the bull. There he stood and hung down his head, and looked so downcast that she began to weep over him.

"What are you weeping for?" asked the bull.

So she told him how the king had come home again, and how the queen had shammed sick and got the doctor to say she could never be well and sound again unless she got some of the blue bull's meat to eat, and now he was to be slaughtered.

Kari Woodenskirt

"If they get me killed first," said the bull, "they'll soon take your life too. Now, if you're of my mind, we'll start off, and go away tonight."

Well, the king's daughter thought it bad, you may be sure, to go and leave her father, but she thought it still worse to be in the house with the queen; and so she gave her word to the bull to go with him.

At night, when all had gone to bed, the king's daughter stole down to the byre to the bull. He took her on his back, and set off as fast as ever he could. And when the folk got up at cockcrow next morning to slaughter the bull, why, he was gone. And when the king got up and asked for his daughter, she was gone too. He sent out messengers on all sides to hunt for them, and gave out notices in all the parish churches; but there was no one who had caught a glimpse of them. Meanwhile, the bull went through many lands with the king's daughter on his back, and so one day they came to a great copper wood, where all the trees, and branches, and leaves, and flowers, and everything, were nothing but copper.

But before they went into the wood, the bull said to the king's daughter:

"Now, when we get into this wood, mind you take care not to touch even a leaf of it, else it's all over both with me and you, for here dwells a troll with three heads who owns this wood."

No, bless her, she'd be sure to take care not to touch anything. She was very careful, and leaned this way and that to miss the boughs, and put them gently aside with her hands; but it was such a thick wood, 'twas scarce possible to get through. And so, with all her pains, somehow or other she tore off a leaf, which she held in her hand.

"Au! Au! What have you done now?" said the bull. "There's nothing for it now but to fight for life or death, but mind you keep the leaf and hide it well."

Soon after, they got to the end of the wood, and the troll with three heads came running up.

"Who is this that touches my wood?" said the troll.

"It's just as much mine as yours," said the bull.

"We'll fight and see," said the troll.

"All right with me," said the bull.

So they rushed at one another and fought. And the bull, he butted and gored and kicked with all his might and main; but the troll gave him as good as he brought, and it lasted the whole day before the bull got the mastery; and then he was so full of wounds, and so worn out, he could scarce lift a leg. They had to stay there a day to rest, and then the bull bade the king's daughter to take the horn of ointment which hung at the troll's belt, and rub him with it. Then he came to himself again, and the next day they set off again. So they travelled many, many days, until after a long long time they came to a silver wood, where all the trees, and branches, and leaves, and flowers, and everything, were of silver.

Before the bull went into the wood, he said to the king's daughter:

"Now, when we get into this wood, for heaven's sake mind you take good care. You mustn't touch anything, and not pluck off so much as one leaf, else it is all over both with me and you; for here is a troll with six heads who owns it, and him I don't think I should be able to master."

"No," said the king's daughter, "I'll take good care and not touch anything you don't wish me to touch."

But when they got into the wood, it was so close and thick, they could scarce get along. She was as careful as careful could be, and leaned to this side and that to miss the boughs, and put them on one side with her hands, but every minute the branches struck her across the eyes, and in spite of all her pains, it so happened she tore off a leaf.

"Au! Au! What have you done now?" said the bull. "There's nothing for it now but to fight for life and death, for this troll has six heads, and is twice as strong as the other. But mind you keep the leaf safe, and hide it well."

Just as he said that, up came the troll.

"Who is this," he said, "that touches my wood?"

"It's as much mine as yours," said the bull.

"We'll fight and see," roared the troll.

"That's all right with me," said the bull, and rushed at the troll, and gored out his eyes, and drove his horns right through his body so that the entrails gushed out. But the troll was almost a match for him, and it lasted three whole days before the troll got the life gored out of him. But then the bull, too, was so weak and wretched it was as much as he could do to stir a limb, and so full of wounds that the blood streamed from him. So he said to the king's daughter, she must take the horn of ointment that hung at the troll's belt and rub him with it. This she did and so he recovered, but they were forced to stay there a week to rest before the bull had strength enough to go on.

At last they set off again, but the bull was still poorly, and they went rather slowly at first. The king's daughter wanted to spare the bull and said that as she was young and light of foot, she could very well walk, but she couldn't get leave to do that. No, she must seat herself up on his back again. So on they travelled through many lands a long time, and the king's daughter did not know in the least whither they went. But after a long, long time they came to a golden wood. It was so grand, the gold dropped from every twig, and all the trees, and boughs, and flowers, and leaves were of pure gold. Here the same thing happened that had happened in the silver wood and copper wood. The bull told the king's daughter she mustn't touch it for anything, for there was a troll with nine heads who owned this wood. He was much bigger and stronger than both the others put together, and the bull didn't think he could get the better of him. No, she'd be sure to take heed not to touch it; that he might know very well. But when they got into the wood, it was far thicker and closer than the silver wood, and the deeper they went into it, the worse it got. The wood went on, getting thicker and thicker, and closer and closer, and at last she thought there was no way at all to get through it. She was so afraid of plucking off anything that she bent and turned herself this way and that, and hither and thither, to keep clear of the boughs, and she pushed them softly away with her hands. But every moment the branches struck her across the eyes, so that she couldn't see what she was clutching at; and lo! before she knew how it came about, she had a golden apple in her hand. She was so bitterly sorry, she burst into tears, and wanted to throw it away; but the bull said she must keep it safe and hide it well, and comforted her as well as he could. But he thought it would be a hard tussle, and he doubted how it would go.

Just then up came the troll with the nine heads, and he looked so terrible the king's daughter scarcely dared to glance at him.

"Who is this that touches my wood?" he roared.

"It's just as much mine as yours," said the bull.

"We'll fight and see," roared the troll.

"All right with me," said the bull. And they rushed at one another and fought, and it was such a dreadful sight the king's daughter was ready to swoon away. The bull gored out the troll's eyes, and drove his horns through and through his body till the entrails came tumbling out; but the troll fought bravely, and when the bull got one head gored to death, the rest breathed life into it again. And so it lasted a whole week before the bull was able to get the life out of them all. But then he was utterly worn out and wretched. He couldn't stir a foot, and his body was all one wound. He couldn't so much as ask the king's daughter to take the horn of ointment which hung at the troll's belt, and rub it over him. But she did it all the same, and then he came to himself again; but they had to lie there and rest three weeks before he was fit to go any further.

Then they set off again, slowly, for the bull said they had still some way to go, and they passed through woods and over many mountain ridges. So after a while they got up into the mountains.

"Do you see anything?" asked the bull.

"No, I see nothing but the sky and the wild mountains," said the king's daughter.

When they got still higher up, the mountain got smoother, and they could see further off.

"Do you see anything now?" asked the bull.

"Yes, I see a small castle far, far away," said the king's daughter.

"It is not as small as it seems from here," said the bull.

At long last they came to a great hillock behind which there was a sheer mountain wall.

"Do you see anything now?" said the bull.

"Yes, now I see the castle close by," said the king's daughter, "and now it is much, much bigger."

"Thither you're to go," said the bull. "Right underneath the castle is a pig-sty, where you are to dwell. When you go thither, you'll find a wooden skirt. Put that on and go up to the castle and say your name is Kari Woodenskirt and ask for a place. But before you go, you must take your little knife and cut my head off, and then you must flay me, and roll up the hide, and lay it under the mountain wall yonder, and thrust the copper leaf and the silver leaf and the golden apple into the hide. At the mountain wall there stands a stick. Whenever you want me you've only got to knock on the wall of rock with that stick."

At first she would not; but the bull said it was the only thanks he would have for what he had done for her, and she could not refuse any more. It hurt her very badly, but she hacked and cut away with her knife at the big beast till she got both his head and his hide off. Then she rolled it up, thrust the copper leaf, the silver leaf, and the golden apple inside it, and put it under the mountain wall.

When she had done that, she went over to the pig-sty, but all the while she wept and grieved. There she put on the wooden skirt and went up to the palace. When she got to the kitchen, she begged for a place and told them her name was Kari Woodenskirt.

"Yes," said the cook, "you may stay here and wash dishes, for the lassie who did that work before has just gone away. But as soon as you get weary of the work, you'll go your way too, I'll be bound."

No, she was sure she wouldn't do that.

She was both quick and neat at washing dishes. When Sunday came, there were to be guests at the palace, and Kari asked if she might have leave to carry up water for the prince, but all the rest laughed at her and said:

"What should you do there? Do you think the prince will glance at you, the way you look?"

But she wouldn't give it up, and kept on begging and praying and at last she got leave. When she ran up the stairs, her wooden skirt made such a clatter the prince came out and asked:

"Who are you?"

"I am just bringing up washing water for you," said Kari.

"Do you really think I want to wash myself in the water you carry?" said the prince, and threw the water over her.

So she had to put up with that, but then she asked leave to go to church. Well, she got that leave too, for the church lay close by. But, first of all, she went to the mountain wall and knocked on its face with the stick which stood there, just as the bull had said. And straightway out came a man and asked what she wanted.

So the princess said she had got leave to go to church and hear the parson preach, but she had no clothes to go in. So he brought out a dress, which was as bright as the copper wood, and she got a horse and saddle besides. When she got to the church, she was so lovely and grand all wondered who she could be, and scarce one of them listened to what the parson said, for they all looked too much at her. The prince himself liked her so much that he didn't take his eyes off her for a single moment.

So, as she went out of the church, the prince ran after her and closed the church door behind her and got one of her gloves. When she went away and mounted her horse, the prince went up to her again and asked whence she came.

"I'm from Washingland," said Kari, and when the prince took out the glove to give it to her, she said:

> In front of me light, and dark at my back,
> So the prince can't see to follow my track.

The prince had never seen the like of that glove, and went about far and wide asking after the land whence the proud lady, who rode off without her glove, said she came; but there was no one who could tell where that land lay.

Next Sunday someone had to go up to the prince with a towel.

"Oh, please let me go up with it!" said Kari.

Kari Woodenskirt

"What's the good of your going?" said the other maid. "You saw how it fared with you last time."

But Kari wouldn't give in. She kept on begging and praying till she got leave, and then she ran up the stairs, so her wooden skirt clattered. Out came the prince, and when he saw it was Kari, he tore the towel out of her hand and threw it into her face.

"Pack yourself off, you ugly troll!" he cried. "Do you think I'd have a towel which you have touched with your smutty fingers?"

After that the prince set off to church, and Kari begged for leave to go too. They all asked why she wanted to go to church—she, who had nothing to put on but that wooden skirt, which was so sooty and ugly. But Kari said she thought the parson preached so well, it did her so much good to listen to him; and so she at last got leave. Now she went again to the rock and knocked, and out came the man and gave her a dress still more beautiful than the first one. It was all covered with silver and it shone like the silver wood. And she got a noble steed besides, with a saddle-cloth broidered with silver, and a silver bit.

When the king's daughter got to the church, the folk were still standing about in the churchyard. And all wondered and wondered who she could be, and the prince was soon on the spot, and came and wished to hold her horse for her while she got off. But she jumped down and said there was no need, for her horse was so well broke, it stood still when she bade it, and came when she called it. So they all went into church; but there was scarce a soul that listened to what the parson said, for they looked at her a deal too much. And the prince fell still deeper in love than the first time.

When the sermon was over, and she went out of church and was going to mount her horse, up came the prince again and asked her whence she came.

"Oh, I'm from Towelland!" said the king's daughter; and as she said that, she dropped her riding-whip, and when the prince stooped to pick it up, she said:

> In front of me light, and dark at my back,
> So the prince can't see to follow my track.

Kari Woodenskirt

So away she went again, and the prince couldn't tell what had become of her. He went about far and wide asking after the land whence she said she came, but there was no one who could tell him where it lay; and so the prince had to give up his search.

Next Sunday someone had to go up to the prince with a comb. Kari begged for leave to go up with it, but the others put her in mind how she had fared the last time, and scolded her for wishing to go before the prince—such a sooty and ugly fright as she was in her wooden skirt. But she wouldn't leave off asking till they let her go up to the prince with his comb. When she came clattering up the stairs again, out came the prince, and took the comb and threw it at her, and bade her be off as fast as she could. After that the prince went to church, and Kari begged for leave to go too. They asked again what she wanted there, she who was so foul and black and who had no clothes to show herself in. Might be the prince or someone else would see her, and then both she and all the others would smart for it; but Kari said they had something else to do than to look at her, and she didn't stop begging and praying till they gave her leave to go.

So the same thing happened now as had happened twice before. She went to the mountain wall and knocked with the stick, and then the man came out and gave her a dress which was far grander than either of the others. It was almost all pure gold, and studded with precious stones; and she got besides a noble steed, with a gold broidered saddle-cloth and a golden bit.

Now when the king's daughter got to the church, there stood the parson and all the people in the churchyard waiting for her. Up came the prince running and wanted to hold her horse, but she jumped off, and said:

"No, thanks, there's no need, for my horse is so well broke, it stands still when I bid him."

So they all hastened into church, and the parson got into the pulpit, but no one listened to a word he said, for they all looked too much at her, and wondered whence she came. And the prince, he was far deeper in love than either of the former times. He had no eyes, or ears, or sense for anything but just to sit and stare at her.

When the sermon was over, and the king's daughter was to go out of the church, the prince let a firkin of pitch be poured upon the porch, that he might come and help her over it; but she didn't care a bit—she put her foot down into the midst of the pitch and jumped across it; but then one of her golden shoes stuck fast in it, and as she got on her horse, the prince came running and asked whence she came.

"From Combland," said Kari. But when the prince wanted to reach her the gold shoe, she said:

> In front of me light, and dark at my back,
> So the prince can't see to follow my track.

So the prince couldn't tell still what had become of her, and he went about a weary time all over the world asking for "Combland"; but when no one could tell him where it lay, he ordered it to be given out every-where that he would wed the girl whose foot could fit the gold shoe.

So many came of all sorts from all sides, fair and ugly alike; but there was no one who had so small a foot as to be able to get on the gold shoe. And after a long, long time, who should come but Kari's wicked step-mother, and her daughter too, and her the gold shoe fitted; but ugly she was, and so loathly she looked, the prince only kept his word sore against his will. Still they got ready the wedding-feast, and she was dressed up and decked out as a bride; but when they rode to church, there sat a little bird in a tree and sang:

> A bit off her heel,
> And a bit off her toe;
> Kari Woodenskirt's shoe
> Is full of blood.

And, sure enough, when they looked to it the bird told the truth, for blood was dripping out of the shoe.

Then all the maids and women who were about the palace had to go up to try on the shoe, but there was none of them whom it would fit at all.

114

Kari Woodenskirt

"But where's Kari Woodenskirt?" asked the prince, when all the rest had tried the shoe, for he understood the song of birds very well and bore in mind what the little bird had said.

"Oh, she, think of that!" said the rest. "It's no good her coming forward. Why, she has feet like a horse."

"Very true, I dare say," said the prince, "but since all the others have tried, Kari may as well try too."

"Kari," he bawled out through the door; and Kari came tramping upstairs, and her wooden skirt clattered as if a whole regiment of dragoons were charging up.

"Now you must try the shoe on, and be a princess, you too," said the other maids, and laughed and made game of her.

Kari took up the shoe, and put her foot into it like nothing, and threw off her wooden skirt; and there she stood in her gold dress, and it shone so that the sunbeams glistened from her. And, lo! on her other foot she had the fellow to the gold shoe.

The prince knew her at once and he grew so glad, he ran up to her and threw his arms round her and gave her a kiss; and when he heard she was a king's daughter, he got gladder still, and then came the wedding-feast. And so

Snip, snap, snout,
And now the tale is out.

Why the Bear Is Stumpy-Tailed

ONE day the Bear met the Fox, who came slinking along with a string of fish he had stolen.

"Where did you get those?" asked the Bear.

"Oh, my Lord Bruin, I've been out fishing and caught them," said the Fox.

So the Bear had a mind to learn to fish too, and bade the Fox tell him how he was to set about it.

"Oh, it's an easy craft for you," answered the Fox, "and soon learned. You've only got to go upon the ice, and cut a hole and stick your tail down into it; and so you must go on holding it there as long as you can. You're not to mind if your tail smarts a little; that's when the fish bite. The longer you hold it there the more fish you'll get; and then all at once out with it, with a cross pull sideways, and with a strong pull too."

Yes, the Bear did as the Fox had said, and held his tail a long, long time down in the hole, till it was fast frozen in. Then he pulled it out with a cross pull, and it snapped off short. That's why Bruin goes about with a stumpy tail to this very day.

East of the Sun
and West of the Moon

ONCE on a time there was a poor peasant who had his hut full of children and not much to give them, either of food or of clothes. Pretty children they all were, but the prettiest was the youngest daughter. She was so lovely there was no end to her loveliness.

So it was on a Thursday night, late in the fall of the year, the sky was cloudy and it was very dark, and it rained and stormed so the walls of the hut creaked and groaned. There they all sat round the fire busy with this thing and that, when all at once something gave three taps at the windowpane. The father went out to see what it was, and when he got out, what should he see but a great big white bear.

"Good evening to you," said the white bear.

"Good evening," said the man.

"If you will give me your youngest daughter, I'll make you as rich as you now are poor," said the bear.

Well, the man liked the thought very much of getting so rich, but still he thought he had to talk with his daughter first; so he went in and told her that there was a great white bear waiting outside, who had promised to make them so rich, if only he could have her. She said no, and refused it outright, so the man went out and settled it with the white bear, that he should come again next Thursday night and get an answer. Meanwhile he talked his daughter over and didn't give her any peace, and kept on talking and telling her of all the riches they would get and how well off she would be herself. And so, at last, she thought better of it, washed and mended her rags, made herself as pretty as she could, and was ready to set off. I can't say her packing gave her much trouble.

Next Thursday night the white bear came to fetch her. And she got upon his back with her bundle and off they went. When they had gone a bit of the way the white bear said:

"Are you afraid?"

No, she wasn't.

"Well, hold tight by my shaggy coat, and then there is nothing to fear," said the bear.

So she rode and she rode a long, long way, till at last they came to a steep mountain. The white bear gave a knock on the mountain, a gate opened, and they went into a castle. All the rooms were lit up, rooms gleaming with gold and with silver, and they came into a huge room where there was a table ready laid. All was as grand as grand could be. Then the white bear gave her a silver bell; when she wanted anything she was only to ring it, and she would get it at once.

Well, when she had eaten, and evening wore on, she grew sleepy after her journey and thought she would like to go to bed. So she rang the bell, and she had hardly touched it before she found herself in a bedroom where there was a bed made, as pretty a bed as anybody could wish to sleep in, with silk pillows and curtains and golden fringes. All that was in the room was of gold or silver. But when she had gone to bed and put out the light, a man came in and laid himself beside her. That was the white bear, who threw off his beast shape at night. But she never saw him, for he always came after she had put out the light and before it dawned he was off again.

So things went on happily for a while, but then she began to get silent and sad; for there she went about all day alone and longed to go home to see her father and mother and sisters and brothers. So one day, when the white bear asked what ailed her, she answered that she felt so forlorn—she was alone all the time, and she longed to go home and see her parents and sisters and brothers, and that was why she was so sad and sorrowful, because she couldn't get to them.

"Perhaps that might be done," said the white bear, "but you must promise me not to talk alone with your mother but only when the rest are by to hear; for she will take you by the hand," he said, "and try to lead you into a room alone to talk, but that you mustn't do, or you'll make us both unhappy."

So, one Sunday the white bear came and said that now they could set off to see her father and mother. Well, off they started, she sitting on his back, and they went far and long. At last they came to a great white house; there her sisters and brothers were running about out of doors at play, and everything was so pretty it was a joy to behold. "That is where your parents live now," said the white bear, "but mind what I have told you, else you'll make us both unhappy."

No, bless her, she wouldn't forget what he had told her; and when they reached the house, the white bear turned right about and left her.

When she came in, there was such joy there was no end to it. None of them thought they could thank her enough for all she had done for them. Now they had everything they wished, as good as good could be, and they all wanted to know how she got on where she lived. She said it was very good to live where she did; she had all she wished. What else she answered I can't say for sure, but I don't believe any of them got very much out of her. But then, in the afternoon when they had finished their dinner, all happened as the white bear had said: the mother wanted to talk to her alone in the bedroom, but she minded what the white bear had said, and wouldn't by any means.

"What we have to talk about, we can just as well talk about here," she said. But somehow or other the mother got round her at last, and she had to tell her the whole story. So she told how every night, when she had gone to bed, a man came and lay down beside her as soon as she had put out the light, and how she never saw him, because he was always up and away before the morning dawned. She grieved much for that, for she thought she'd so like to see him, and how all day long she walked about there alone and how very lonesome she was.

"Oh, dear, oh, dear, it may well be a troll you are sharing your bed with!" said the mother. "But now I'll tell you how to set eyes on him. I'll give you a bit of candle, which you can carry home in your bosom;

just light that while he is asleep, but take care not to drop the tallow on him."

Yes, she took the candle and hid it in her bosom, and as night drew on the white bear came and fetched her away.

When they had gone a bit of the way the white bear asked if all hadn't happened as he had said. Well, she couldn't say it hadn't. "Now, mind," said he, "if you have listened to your mother's advice you have made us both unhappy, and all is finished between us."

"Oh, no," she said, she hadn't listened to her mother's advice.

When she reached home and had gone to bed, it was the old story over again; there came a man and lay down beside her. But at dead of night, when she heard that he slept, she got up and lit the candle, and let the light shine on him, and so she saw that he was the handsomest prince one ever set eyes on, and she got so fond of him that she thought she couldn't live if she didn't give him a kiss there and then. And so she did, but just as she kissed him she dropped three hot drops of tallow on his shirt, and he woke up.

"What have you done?" he cried. "Now you have made us both unhappy. Had you held out only this one year you would have set me free; for I have a stepmother who has bewitched me, so I am a white bear by day and a man by night. But now all ties are snapped between us, now I must leave you and go back to her. She lives in a castle that stands East of the Sun and West of the Moon, and there is a princess with a nose three yards long, and she is the one I must now take for wife."

She wept and grieved, but there was no help for it; go he must.

Then she asked if she mightn't go with him.

No, she mightn't.

"Tell me the way then, and I'll search you out; that surely I may get leave to do," she said.

Yes, that she might do, but there was no way to that place. It just lay East of the Sun and West of the Moon, and thither she'd never find her way.

So, next morning when she woke up, both prince and castle were gone. She lay in a little green glade in the midst of the dark, dense forest, and by her side lay the bundle of rags she had brought with her from home.

When she had rubbed the sleep out of her eyes and had wept till she was tired, she set out on her way and walked many, many days, till she came to a steep mountain wall. Under the mountain sat an old hag and played with a golden apple. Her the lassie asked if she knew the way to the prince, who lived with his stepmother in the castle that lay East of the Sun and West of the Moon, and who was to wed a princess with a nose three yards long.

"How did you come to know about him?" asked the old hag. "But maybe you are the lassie who ought to have had him?"

Yes, she was.

"So, so, it is you, is it?" said the old hag. "Well, all I know about him is that he lives in the castle that lies East of the Sun and West of the Moon, and thither you'll come late or never. But I'll lend you my horse; on him you can ride to my next neighbour; maybe she'll be able to tell you. And when you get there, just give the horse a switch under the left ear and tell him to be off home. And wait, this golden apple you may take with you," said the old hag.

So the lassie got up on the horse and rode a long, long time, till she came to another mountain, under which sat another old hag with a golden carding comb.

Her the lassie asked if she knew the way to the castle that lay East of the Sun and West of the Moon. She answered like the first old hag— that she knew nothing about it, except it was East of the Sun and West of the Moon.

"And thither you'll come late or never, but I'll lend you my horse to my next neighbour; maybe she'll be able to tell you. And when you get there, just switch the horse under the left ear, and tell him to be off home."

And then she gave her the golden carding comb. It might be she'd find a use for it, she said.

East of the Sun and West of the Moon

So the lassie got on the horse and rode a far, far way and a weary time; and so at last she came to another huge mountain, under which sat an old hag spinning with a golden spinning wheel. Her, too, she asked if she knew the way to the prince, and knew where the castle was that lay East of the Sun and West of the Moon. But it was the same thing over.

"Maybe you are the one who ought to have had the prince?" asked the old hag.

Yes, it was.

But she didn't know the way a bit better than the other two. East of the Sun and West of the Moon it was, she knew, that was all.

"And thither you'll come late or never," she said, "but I'll lend you my horse, and then I think you had better ride to the East Wind and ask him; maybe he knows where it is and can blow you thither. When you get to him, you need only give the horse a switch under the left ear, and he'll trot home of himself again." And then she gave her the golden spinning wheel. "Maybe you'll find a use for it," said the old hag.

Then on rode the lassie, many days, a weary time, before she got to the East Wind's house, but at last she did reach it, and then she asked the East Wind if he could tell her the way to the prince who lived in the castle that lay East of the Sun and West of the Moon.

Yes, the East Wind had heard of the prince, and of the castle too, but he couldn't tell the way, for he had never blown so far.

"But if you will," he said, "I'll take you to my brother, the West Wind. Maybe he knows, for he is much stronger. Sit on my back and I'll carry you thither."

Yes, she got on his back, and I should think they went briskly along. When they got there, they went in and the East Wind said that the lass he had brought was the one who ought to have had the prince who lived in the castle East of the Sun and West of the Moon; and so she had set out to seek him, and how he had come with her, and would be glad to know if the West Wind knew the way to the castle.

"Nay," said the West Wind, "so far I have never blown, but if you will I'll take you to the South Wind, for he is much stronger than either of us, and he has travelled far and wide; maybe he can tell you. You can get on my back, and I'll carry you to him."

Yes, she got on his back and so they travelled to the South Wind, and I should say they weren't a long time on the way.

When they got there, the West Wind asked him if he could tell the lassie the way to the castle that lay East of the Sun and West of the Moon. "It was she who ought to have had the prince there," he said.

"You don't say so! Is she the one?" said the South Wind. "I have surely been to many places in my time, but that far I have never blown. But if you will, I'll take you to my brother, the North Wind; he is the oldest and the strongest of the whole lot of us. If he doesn't know where it is, you'll never find anyone in the world to tell you. You can get on my back, and I'll carry you thither."

Yes, she got on his back and away he went at full speed. They weren't long on their way.

When they got to the North Wind's house, he was so wild and cross that cold puffs came from him a long way off. "Blast you both, what do you want?" he roared out to them ever so far off, so that it struck them with an icy shiver.

"Well," said the South Wind, "you needn't be so severe and hard on us, for here am I, your brother, the South Wind, and here is the lassie who ought to have had the prince who dwells in the castle that lies East of the Sun and West of the Moon, and now she wants to ask you if you ever were there and if you can tell her the way, for she wants so much to find him again."

"Yes, I know well enough where it is," said the North Wind. "Once in my life I blew an aspen-leaf thither, then I was so worn out and tired I couldn't blow a puff for ever so many days afterwards. But if you really wish to go thither and are not afraid to come along with me, I'll take you on my back and see if I can blow you thither."

Yes, with all her heart she must and would get thither if it were possible in any way; and as for fear, however madly it went, she wouldn't be at all afraid.

"Well, well, then you must sleep here tonight," said the North Wind, "for we must have a whole day before us if we are to get thither at all."

Early next morning the North Wind woke her and puffed himself up, and blew himself out, and made himself so stout and big 'twas gruesome to look at him. And off they went, high up through the air, as if they would never stop till they got to the world's end.

Down below there was such a storm that houses and long tracts of wood were torn up; and when it swept over the great sea, hundreds of ships went down. So they tore on and on—no one can believe how far they went—and all the while they still went over the sea, and the North Wind got more and more weary and so out of breath he could scarce bring out a puff. Deeper and deeper down he drooped, till at last he sank so low that the crests of the waves washed about the lassie's heels.

"Are you afraid?" said the North Wind. "No," she said.

But they weren't far from land, and the North Wind had just so much strength left in him that he managed to throw her up on the shore under the windows of the castle that lay East of the Sun and West of the Moon. But then he was so weak and worn out, he had to stay there and rest for many days before he could get home again.

Next morning the lassie sat down under the castle's window, and began to play with the golden apple; and the first person she saw was the long-nose, who was to have the prince.

"What do you want for your golden apple, you lassie?" she said, and stuck her nose out of the window.

"It's not for sale for gold or money," answered the lassie.

"If it isn't for sale for gold or money, what is it then you'll sell it for? You may name your own price," said the princess.

"Well, if I may get to the prince who lives here and stay with him overnight, you shall have it," said the lassie, whom the North Wind had brought.

Yes, she might, that could be done.

So the princess got the golden apple. But when the lassie came up to the prince's room at night, he was fast asleep; she called him and shook him and between whiles she wept. But do what she might, she couldn't wake him up, for they had given him a sleeping draught in the evening.

Next morning, as soon as the day broke, came the princess with the long nose, and drove her out again.

So, in the daytime, she sat down under the castle windows, and began to card with her golden carding comb, and the same thing happened. The princess asked what she wanted for it, and she said it wasn't for sale for gold or money, but if she might get leave to go up to the prince and stay overnight with him, the princess should have it.

But when she went up, she found him fast asleep again; and for all she called, and all she shook, and all she wept and prayed, she couldn't get life into him. And as soon as the first grey peep of day came, then came the princess with the long nose and chased her out again.

In the daytime the lassie sat down outside under the castle windows and began to spin with her golden spinning wheel, and that, too, the princess with the long nose wanted to have. She threw up the window and asked what she wanted for it. The lassie said as she had said twice before—it wasn't for sale for gold or money, but if she might go up to the prince who was there and stay by him overnight, she might have it.

Yes, she might do that, and welcome. But now you must know there were some Christian folk who had been carried off thither, and as they sat in their room, which was next to the prince's, they had heard how a woman had been in there and had wept and cried and called him two nights running, and they told that to the prince.

That evening when the princess came with her sleeping draught, the prince made as if he drank, but threw it behind his shoulder, for he could guess it was a sleepy drink.

So, when the lassie came in, she found him wide awake, and then she told him the whole story of how she had come thither.

"You have just come in the very nick of time," said the prince, "for tomorrow is to be our wedding day; but I don't want to have the long-nose for bride, and you are the only one who can set me free. I'll say I want to see what my bride is fit for, and ask her to wash the shirt which has the three spots of tallow on it. She'll say yes, for she doesn't know it was you who put them there. But that is a work only for Christian folk, and not for such a pack of trolls; and so I'll say that I won't have any other for my bride than the one who can do it, and you can, I know that."

So there was great joy and happiness between them, all that night. But the next day, when the wedding was to be, the prince said:

"First of all I'd like to see what my bride is fit for."

"Yes," said the stepmother, with all her heart.

"Well," said the prince, "I have got a fine shirt which I'd like for my wedding shirt, but somehow or other it has got three spots of tallow on it, which I must have washed out. And I have sworn never to take any other bride than the one who is able to do that. If she can't, she isn't worth having."

Well, that was no great thing, they said, so they agreed, and she with the long nose began to wash away as hard as she could. But the more she rubbed and scrubbed, the bigger grew the spots.

"You can't wash," said the old hag, her mother. "Come, let me try."

But she hadn't long taken the shirt in her hand before it got far worse than ever, and with all her rubbing and wringing and scrubbing, the spots grew bigger and blacker, and the blacker and uglier was the shirt.

Then all the other trolls began to wash, but the longer it lasted the blacker and uglier the shirt grew, till at last it was as black all over as if it had been up the chimney.

"You are none of you worth a straw," said the prince. "You can't wash. Why, there outside sits a beggar lassie, and I'll be bound she knows how to wash better than the whole lot of you. Come in, you, lassie," he called.

Well, in she came.

"Can you wash this shirt clean, lassie, you?" said he.

"Oh, I don't know," she said, "but I'll try."

And almost before she had taken it and dipped it in the water, it was white as driven snow and whiter still.

"Yes, you are the one I want for my bride," said the prince.

At that the old troll-hag flew into such a rage, she burst on the spot, and the princess with the long nose after her, and the whole pack of trolls after her—at least I have never heard a word about them since.

The prince and his bride then set free all the poor Christian folk who had been carried off and shut up there. Then they took with them all the silver and gold they could carry, and moved away as far as they could from the castle that lay East of the Sun and West of the Moon.

The Three Princesses
in the Mountain So Blue

THERE were once upon a time a king and queen who had no children, and they took it so much to heart that they hardly ever had a happy moment. One day the king stood at his doorstep and looked out over the fields and meadows and all that was his. He had plenty and more than that, both of goods and of ground, but not even this could make him happy, since he did not know what would become of it all after his time. As he stood there pondering, an old hag who went about begging a trifle in heaven's name came up to him. She greeted him and curtsied, and asked what ailed the king, since he looked so sad.

"You can't do anything to help me, my good woman," said the king. "It's no use telling you."

"I am not so sure about that," said the beggar woman. "Very little is wanted when luck is in the way. The king is thinking that he has no heir to his crown and kingdom, but he need not mourn on that account," she said. "The queen shall have three daughters, but great care must be taken that they do not come out under the open heavens before they are all fifteen years old; otherwise a snowflake will come and carry them away."

When the time came, the queen had a beautiful baby girl; the year after she had another; and the third year she also had a girl.

The king and queen were glad beyond all measure; but though the king was very happy, he did not forget to set a watch in front of the door, so that the princesses should not get out.

As they grew up, they became both fair and beautiful, and all went well with them in every way. Their only sorrow was that they were not allowed to go out and play like other children. For all they begged and prayed their parents and for all they besought the sentinel, it was of no avail; go out they must not, before they were fifteen years old, all of them.

Then one day, not long before the fifteenth birthday of the youngest princess, there was such beautiful weather. The king and the queen were out driving, and the princesses were standing at the window looking out. The sun was shining, and everything looked so green and beautiful that they felt that they must go out, happen what might. So they begged and entreated and urged the sentinel, all three of them, that he should let them down into the garden. He could see for himself how warm and fair it was; no snowy weather could come on such a day. Well, he didn't think it looked much like it either, and if they must go they had better go, the soldier said. But it must be for only a minute, and he himself would go with them and look after them.

When they got down into the garden, they ran up and down, and filled their laps with flowers and green leaves, the prettiest they could find. At last they could carry no more, but just as they were going indoors they caught sight of a large rose at the other end of the garden. It was many times prettier than any they had gathered, so they must have that also. But just as they bent down to take the rose, a big dense snowflake came and carried them away.

There was great mourning over the whole country, and the king made known from all the churches that anyone who could save the princesses should have half the kingdom and his golden crown and whichever princess he liked to choose.

You can well understand there were plenty who wanted to gain half the kingdom, and a princess into the bargain. Off they set, both lords and lads, for the corners of the kingdom. But there was no one who could find the princesses, or even get any tidings of them.

When all the grand and rich people in the country had had their turn, a captain and a lieutenant came to the palace and wanted to try

their luck. Oh, yes, the king fitted them out both with silver and gold, and wished them success on their journey.

Then came a soldier, who lived with his mother in a little cottage some way from the palace. He had dreamed one night that he also was trying to find the princesses. When the morning came, he still remembered what he had dreamed, and told his mother about it.

"Some witchery must have got hold of you," said the woman, "but you must dream the same thing three nights running, else there is nothing in it." And the next two nights the same thing happened; he had the same dream, and he felt he must go. So he washed himself and put on his uniform, and went into the king's kitchen. It was the day after the captain and the lieutenant had set out.

"You had better go home again," said the king; "the princesses are beyond your reach, I should say; and besides, I have spent so much money on outfits that I have nothing left today. You had better come back another time."

"If I go, I must go today," said the soldier. "Money I do not want. I only need a drop in my flask and some food in my knapsack," he said; "but it must be a good sackful—as much meat and bacon as I can carry."

Yes, that he might have, if that was all he wanted.

So he set off, and he had not gone many miles before he overtook the captain and the lieutenant.

"Where are you going?" asked the captain, when he saw the man in uniform.

"I'm going to try if I can find the king's daughters," answered the soldier.

"So are we," said the captain, "and since your errand is the same, you may keep company with us, for if we don't find them, you are not likely to find them either, my lad," said he.

When they had gone awhile, the soldier left the high road and took a path into the forest.

"Where are you going?" said the captain. "It is best to follow the highway."

The Three Princesses in the Mountain So Blue

"That may be," said the soldier, "but this is my way."

He kept to the path, and when the others saw this, they turned round and followed him. Away they went further and further, far across big forests and along narrow valleys.

And at last it became lighter, and when they had got out of the forest altogether, they came to a long foot-bridge, which they had to cross. But on that bridge a bear stood on guard. He rose on his hind-legs and came towards them as if he wanted to eat them.

"What shall we do now?" said the captain.

"They say that the bear is fond of meat," said the soldier, and then he threw a fore quarter to him, and so they got past. But when they reached the other end of the bridge, there stood a lion, which came roaring towards them with open jaws as if he wanted to swallow them.

"I think we had better turn right-about. We shall never be able to get past him alive," said the captain.

"Oh, I don't think he is so very dangerous," said the soldier. "I have heard that lions are very fond of pork, and I have half a pig in my knapsack." And then he threw a ham to the lion, who began eating and gnawing, and thus they got past him also.

In the evening they came to a fine big house. Each room was more gorgeous than the other; all was glitter and splendour wherever they looked; but that did not satisfy their hunger. The captain and the lieutenant went round rattling their money, and wanted to buy some food. But they saw no people nor could they find a crumb of food in the house. So the soldier offered them some food from his knapsack, which they were not too proud to accept, nor did they want any pressing. They helped themselves of what he had as if they had never tasted food before.

The next day the captain said they would have to go out shooting and try to get something to live upon. Close to the house was a large forest where there were plenty of hares and birds. The lieutenant was to remain at home and tend the house and cook the food that remained in the soldier's knapsack. In the meantime the captain and the soldier shot so much game that they were hardly able to carry it home. When they

133

came to the door, they found the lieutenant in such a terrible plight that he was scarcely able to open the door to them.

"What is the matter with you?" said the captain. The lieutenant then told them that as soon as they were gone a tiny old man, with a long beard, who went on crutches, came in and asked so plaintively for a penny. But no sooner had he got it than he let it fall on the floor, and for all he raked and scraped with his crutch he was not able to get hold of it, so stiff and stark was he.

"I pitied the poor old body," said the lieutenant, "and so I bent down to pick up the penny, but then he was neither stiff nor stark any longer. He began to belabour me with his crutches till very soon I was unable to move a limb."

"You ought to be ashamed of yourself! You, one of the king's own men, to let an old cripple give you a thrashing, and then tell people of it into the bargain!" said the captain. "Pshaw! Tomorrow I'll stop at home, and then you'll hear another story."

The next day the lieutenant and the soldier went out shooting and the captain remained at home to cook and tend the house. But if he fared no worse, he certainly fared no better than the lieutenant. In a little while the old man came in and asked for a penny. He let it fall as soon as he got it; gone it was and could not be found. So he asked the captain to help him to find it and the captain, without giving a thought, bent down to look for it. But no sooner was he on his knees than the cripple began belabouring him with his crutches, and every time the captain tried to rise, he got a blow which sent him reeling. When the others came home in the evening, he still lay on the same spot and could neither see nor speak.

The third day the soldier was to remain at home while the other two went out shooting. The captain said he must take care of himself, "for the old fellow will soon put an end to you, my lad," said he.

"Oh, there can't be much life in one if such an old crook can take it," said the soldier.

They were no sooner outside the door than the old man came in and asked for a penny again.

The Three Princesses in the Mountain So Blue

"Money I have never owned," said the soldier, "but food I'll give you, as soon as it is ready. But if we are to get it cooked, you must go and cut the wood."

"That I can't," said the old man.

"If you can't, you must learn," said the soldier. "I will soon show you. Come along with me down to the wood-shed." There he dragged out a heavy log and cut a cleft in it, and drove in a wedge till the cleft deepened.

"Now you must lie down and look right along the cleft, and you'll soon learn how to cut wood," said the soldier. "In the meantime I'll show you how to use the ax."

The old man was dumb enough to do what he was told. He lay down and looked steadily along the log. When the soldier saw the old man's beard had got well into the cleft, he struck out the wedge, the cleft closed, and the old man was caught by the beard. The soldier began to beat him with the ax handle, and then swung the ax round his head, and vowed that he would split his skull if he did not tell him, there and then, where the princesses were.

"Spare my life, spare my life, and I'll tell you!" said the old man. "To the east of the house there is a big mound; on top of the mound you must dig out a square piece of turf, and then you will see a big stone slab. Under that there is a deep hole through which you must let yourself down, and you'll then come to another world, and that's where the mountain trolls are keeping the princesses hidden. But the way is long and dark and it goes through both fire and water."

When the soldier got to know this, he released the old man, who was not long in making off.

When the captain and lieutenant came home, they were surprised to find the soldier alive. Well, he told them what had happened from first to last, where the princesses were and how they should find them. They became as pleased as if they had already found them, and when they had had some food, they took with them a bucket and as much rope as they could find, and all three set off to the mound. There they first dug out the turf just as the old man had told them, and underneath they found a

135

big stone slab, which it took all their strength to turn over. They then began to measure how deep it was; they joined on ropes both two and three times, but they were no nearer the bottom the last time than the first. At last they had to join all the ropes they had, both the coarse and fine, and then they found it reached the bottom.

The captain was, of course, the first who wanted to descend. "But when I tug at the rope you must make haste to drag me up again," he said. He found the way both dark and unpleasant, but he thought he would go on as long as it became no worse. But all at once he felt ice-cold water spouting about his ears. He became frightened to death and began tugging at the rope.

The lieutenant was the next to try, but it fared no better with him. No sooner had he got through the flood of water than he saw a blazing fire yawning beneath him, which so frightened him that he also turned back.

The soldier then got into the bucket, and down he went through fire and water, right on till he came to the bottom, where it was so pitch dark that he could not see his hand before him. He dared not let go the bucket, but went round in a circle, feeling and fumbling about him. At last he discovered a gleam of light far, far away like the dawn of day, and he went on in that direction.

When he had gone a bit, it began to grow light around him, and before long he saw a golden sun rising in the sky there. And then the landscape became bright and pretty, just as it was in the real world.

First he came to some cattle, which were so fat that their hides glistened a long way off. And when he had got past them, he came to a fine, big palace. He walked through many rooms without meeting anybody. At last he heard the hum of a spinning wheel, and when he entered the room, he found the eldest princess sitting there spinning copper yarn. The room and everything in it were of brightly polished copper.

"Oh, dear, oh, dear! What are Christian people doing here?" said the princess. "Heaven preserve you! What do you want?"

"I want to set you free and get you out of the mountain," said the soldier.

"Oh, dear me, leave! If the troll comes home, he will put an end to you at once. He has three heads," said she.

"I do not care if he has four," said the soldier. "I am here, and here I shall remain."

"Well, if you will be so headstrong, I must see if I can help you," said the princess.

She then told him to creep behind the big brewing-vat which stood in the front hall; meanwhile she would receive the troll and scratch his heads till he went to sleep.

"And when I go out and call the hens you must hurry and come in," she said. "But you must first try if you can swing the sword which is lying on the table." No, it was too heavy, he could not even move it. He had then to take a strengthening draught from the horn which hung behind the door; after that he was just able to stir it. So he took another draught, and then he could lift it. So he took a right, big swallow, and he could swing the sword as easily as anything.

All at once the troll came rushing so fast that the palace shook.

"Twee, twee! I smell Christian flesh and blood in my house," said he.

"Yes," answered the princess, "a raven flew past here just now, and in his beak he had a human bone, which he dropped down the chimney. I threw it out and swept and cleaned up after it, but I suppose it still smells."

"So it does," said the troll.

"But come and lie down and I'll scratch your heads," said the princess; "the smell will be gone by the time you wake."

The troll was quite willing, and before long he fell asleep and began snoring. When she saw he was sleeping soundly, she placed some stools and cushions under his heads and went to call the hens. The soldier then stole into the room with the sword, and with one blow cut all the three heads off the troll.

The princess was as pleased as a fiddler, and went with the soldier to her sisters, so that he could also set them free. First they went across a courtyard and then through many long rooms till they came to a big door.

"Here you must enter; here she is," said the princess. When he opened the door, he found himself in a large hall where everything was of pure silver. There sat the second sister at a silver spinning wheel.

"Oh, dear, oh, dear!" she said. "What do you want here?"

"I want to set you free from the troll," said the soldier.

"Oh, dear, oh, dear, just leave," said the princess. "If he finds you here he will take your life on the spot."

"That might well be awkward if I don't take his first," said the soldier.

"Well, since you will stay," she said, "you will have to creep behind the big brewing-vat in the front hall. But you must make haste and come as soon as you hear me calling the hens."

But first he had to try if he was able to swing the troll's sword, which lay on the table; it was much larger and heavier than the first one; he was hardly able to move it. When he had taken three draughts from the horn, he could lift it; and when he had taken three more, he could handle it as if it were a rolling pin.

After a while he heard a heavy, rumbling noise that was quite terrible, and shortly after a troll with six heads came in.

"Twee, twee!" he said as soon as he got his noses inside the door. "I smell Christian blood and bone in my house."

"Yes, just think! A raven came flying past here with a thigh-bone, which he dropped down the chimney," said the princess. "I threw it out, but the raven brought it back again. At last I got rid of it and made haste to clean the room, but I suppose the smell is not quite gone," she said.

"No, I can smell it well," said the troll. But he was tired and put his heads in the princess's lap, and she went on scratching them till they fell a-snoring, all six of them. Then she called the hens, and the soldier came and cut off all the heads as if they were set on cabbage stalks.

She was no less glad than her elder sister, as you may imagine, and danced and sang; but in the midst of their joy they remembered their youngest sister. They went with the soldier across a large courtyard, and, after walking through many, many rooms, he came to the hall of gold where the third sister was.

She sat at a golden spinning wheel spinning gold yarn, and the room from ceiling to floor glistened and glittered till it hurt one's eyes.

"Heaven preserve both you and me. What do you want here?" said the princess. "Go, go, else the troll will kill us both."

"Just as well two as one," answered the soldier. The princess cried and wept, but it was all of no use, he must and would remain. Well, since there was no help for it, he would have to try if he could use the troll's sword on the table in the front hall. But he was only just able to budge it; it was still larger and heavier than the other two swords.

He then had to take the horn down from the wall and take three draughts from it, but was only just able to stir the sword. When he had taken three more draughts, he could lift it; and when he had taken another three, he swung it as easily as if it had been a feather.

The princess then settled with the soldier to do the same as her sisters had done. As soon as the troll was well asleep, she would call the hens, and he must then make haste and come in and put an end to the troll.

All of a sudden they heard such a thundering, rumbling noise, as if the walls and roof were tumbling in.

"Twee, twee! I smell Christian blood and bone in my house," said the troll, sniffing with all his nine noses.

"Yes, you never saw the like! Just now a raven flew past here and dropped a human bone down the chimney. I threw it out, but the raven brought it back, and this went on for some time," said the princess; but she got it burned at last, she said, and she had both swept and cleaned the place, but she supposed it still smelt.

"Yes, I can smell it well," said the troll.

"Come here and lie down in my lap and I will scratch your heads," said the princess. "The smell will be all gone when you awake."

He did so, and when he was snoring at his best, she put stools and cushions under the heads so that she could get away to call the hens. The soldier then came in in his stockinged feet and struck at the troll, so that eight of the heads fell off at one blow. But the sword was too short and did not reach far enough; the ninth head woke up and began to roar.

"Twee, twee! I smell a Christian."

"Yes, here he is," answered the soldier, and before the troll could get up and seize hold of him, the soldier struck him another blow and the last head rolled along the floor.

You can well imagine how glad the princesses became now that they no longer had to sit and scratch the trolls' heads. They did not know how they could do enough for him who had saved them. The youngest princess took off her gold ring and knotted it in his hair. They then took with them as much gold and silver as they thought they could carry, and set off on their way home.

As soon as they tugged at the rope, the captain and the lieutenant pulled up the princesses, the one after the other. But when they were safely up, the soldier thought it was foolish of him not to have gone up before the princesses, for he had not very much belief in his comrades. He thought he would first try them, so he put a heavy lump of gold in the basket and got out of the way. When the basket was halfway up, they cut the rope and the lump of gold fell to the bottom with such a crash that pieces of gold flew about his ears.

"Now we are rid of him," they said, and threatened the princesses with their lives if they did not say that it was they who had saved them from the trolls. They were forced to agree to this, much against their will, and especially the youngest princess. But life was precious, and so the two who were strongest had their way.

When the captain and lieutenant got home with the princesses, you may be sure there were great rejoicings at the palace. The king was so glad he didn't know which leg to stand on; he brought out his best wine from his cupboard and wished the two officers welcome. If they had never been honoured before they were honoured now in full measure, and no mistake. They walked and strutted about the whole of the day, as if they were the cocks of the walk, since they were now going to have the king for father-in-law, for it was understood they should each have whichever of the princesses they liked and half the kingdom between them. They both wanted the youngest princess, but for all they prayed and threatened her it was of no use; she would not hear or listen to either.

They then asked the king if they might have twelve men to watch over her; she was so sad and gloomy since she had been in the mountain that they were afraid she might do something to herself.

Yes, that they might have, and the king himself told the watch they must look after her well and follow her wherever she went and stood.

They then began to prepare for the wedding of the two eldest sisters. It should be such a wedding as never was heard or spoken of before, and there was no end to the brewing and the baking and the slaughtering.

In the meantime the soldier walked and strolled about down in the other world. He thought it was hard that he should see neither people nor daylight any more. But he would have to do something, he thought, and so for many days he went about from room to room and opened all the drawers and cupboards and searched about on the shelves and looked at all the fine things that were there. At last he came to a drawer in a table, in which there lay a golden key. He tried this key in all the locks he could find, but there was none it fitted till he came to a little cupboard over the bed, and in that he found an old rusty whistle. "I wonder if there is any sound in it," he thought, and put it to his mouth. No sooner had he whistled than he heard a whizzing and a whirring from all quarters, and such a large flock of birds swept down that they blackened all the field in which they settled.

"What does our master want today?" they asked.

If he were their master, the soldier said, he would like to know if they could tell him how to get up to the earth again. No, none of them knew anything about that. "But our mother has not yet arrived," they said; "if she can't help you, no one can."

So he whistled once more, and shortly heard something flapping its wings far away, and then it began to blow so hard that he was carried away between the houses and across the courtyard like a wisp of hay.

And if he had not caught hold of the fence, he would no doubt have been blown away altogether.

A big eagle—bigger than you can imagine—then swooped down in front of him.

"You come rather sharply," said the soldier.

"As you whistle so I come," answered the eagle. So he asked her if she knew any means by which he could get away from the world under the ground.

"You can't get away from here unless you can fly," said the eagle, "but if you will slaughter twelve oxen for me, so that I can eat my fill, I will try to help you. Have you got a knife?"

"No, but I have a sword," he said. When the eagle had swallowed the twelve oxen, she asked the soldier to kill one more for victuals on the journey. "Every time I gape, you must be quick and fling a piece into my mouth," she said, "else I shall not be able to carry you up to earth."

He did as she asked him and hung two large bags of meat round her neck and seated himself among her feathers. The eagle then began to flap her wings and off they went through the air like the wind. It was as much as the soldier could do to hold on, and it was with the greatest difficulty he managed to throw the pieces of flesh into the eagle's mouth every time she opened it.

At last the day began to dawn, but the eagle was then almost exhausted and her wings began to droop, but the soldier was prepared and seized the last hind quarter and flung it to her. Then she gained strength and brought him up to earth. When she had sat and rested awhile at the top of a large pine-tree, she set off with him again at such a pace that flashes of lightning were seen both by sea and land wherever they went.

Close to the palace the soldier got off and the eagle flew home again, but first she told him that if he at any time should want her he need only blow the whistle and she would be there at once.

In the meantime everything was ready at the palace, and the time approached when the captain and lieutenant were to be married with the two eldest princesses, who, however, were not much happier than their youngest sister. Scarcely a day passed without weeping and mourning, and the nearer the wedding day approached the more sorrowful did they become.

At last the king asked what was the matter with them. He thought it was very strange that they were not merry and happy, now that they were saved and had been set free and were going to be married. They had to give some answer, and so the eldest sister said they never would be happy any more unless they could get such checkers as they had played with in the mountain so blue.

That, thought the king, could be easily managed, and so he sent word to all the best and cleverest goldsmiths in the country that they should make these checkers for the princesses. For all they tried there was no one who could make them. At last all the goldsmiths had been to the palace except one, and he was an old, frail man who had not done any work for many years, except odd jobs by which he was just able to keep himself alive. To him the soldier went and asked to be apprenticed. The old man was so glad to get him (for he had not had an apprentice for many a day) that he brought out a flask from his chest and sat down to drink with the soldier. Before long the drink got into his head, and when the soldier saw this, he persuaded him to go up to the palace and tell the king that he would undertake to make the checkers for the princesses.

He was ready to do that on the spot. He had made finer and grander things in his day, he said. When the king heard there was someone outside who could make the checkers, he was not long in coming out.

"Is it true what you say, that you can make such checkers as the ones on the mountain so blue?" he asked.

"Yes, it is no lie," said the goldsmith; that he would answer for.

"That's well!" said the king. "Here is the gold to make them with, but if you do not succeed you will lose your life, since you have come and offered yourself; and they must be finished in three days."

The next morning when the goldsmith was himself again, he was not quite so confident about the job. He wailed and wept and scolded his apprentice, who had got him into such a scrape while he was drunk. The best thing would be to make short work of himself at once, he said, for there could be no hope for his life. When the best and grandest goldsmiths could not make such checkers, was it likely that he could do it?

"Don't fret on that account," said the soldier, "but let me have the gold and I'll get the checkers ready in time; but I must have a room to myself to work in," he said. This he got, and thanks into the bargain.

The time wore on, and the soldier did nothing but lounge about, and the goldsmith began to grumble, because he would not begin with the work.

"Don't worry yourself about it," said the soldier, "there is plenty of time! If you are not satisfied with what I have promised, you had better make the checkers yourself." The same thing went on both that day and the next; and when the smith heard neither hammer nor file from the soldier's room the whole of the last day, he quite gave himself up for lost. It was now no use to think any longer about saving his life, he thought.

But when the night came on, the soldier opened the window and blew his whistle. The eagle then came and asked what he wanted.

"Those gold checkers, which the princesses had in the mountain so blue," said the soldier; "but you'll want something to eat first, I suppose? I have two ox carcasses lying ready for you in the hay-loft yonder. You had better finish them," he said. When the eagle had done this, she did not tarry, and long before the sun rose she was back again with the checkers. The soldier then put them under his bed and lay down to sleep.

Early next morning the goldsmith came and knocked at his door.

"What are you after now again?" asked the soldier. "You rush about enough in the day, goodness knows! If one cannot have peace when one is in bed, whoever would be an apprentice here?" said he.

Neither praying nor begging helped that time; the goldsmith must and would come in, and at last he was let in.

And then, you may be sure, there was soon an end to his wailing.

The Three Princesses in the Mountain So Blue

But still more glad than the goldsmith were the princesses, when he came up to the palace with the checkers, and gladdest of all was the youngest princess.

"Have you made them yourself?" she asked.

"No, if I must speak the truth, it is not I," he said, "but my apprentice, who has made them."

"I should like to see that apprentice," said the princess. In fact all three wanted to see him, and if he valued his life, he would have to come.

He was not afraid, either of women or of lords, said the soldier, and if it could be any amusement to them to look at his rags, they should soon have that pleasure.

The youngest princess recognized him at once. She pushed the guard aside and ran up to him, gave him her hand, and said:

"Good day, and thank you for the good time we had together. It is he who freed us from the trolls in the mountain," she said to the king. "He is the one I will have!" and then she pulled off his cap and showed them the ring she had tied in his hair.

It soon came out how the captain and lieutenant had behaved, and so they had to pay the penalty of their treachery with their lives, and that was the end of their grandeur. But the soldier got the golden crown and half the kingdom, and married the youngest princess.

At the wedding they drank and feasted both well and long; for feast they all could, even though they could not save the king's daughters. And if they have not yet done feasting and drinking, they must be at it still.

The Three Bushy Billy-Goats

ONCE on a time there were three billy-goats who were going to the mountains to get fat.

On the way they had to pass over a bridge that led across waterfalls, and under the bridge lived a great ugly troll, with eyes as big as pewter plates and a nose as long as a rake handle.

First came the youngest bushy billy-goat and wanted to cross the bridge.

"Trip, trap; trip, trap! went the bridge.

"WHO'S THAT tripping over my bridge?" roared the troll.

"Oh, it is only I, the smallest bushy billy-goat; and I'm going up to the mountains to make myself fat," said the billy-goat with such a small voice.

"Now, I'm coming for you," said the troll.

"Oh no, please don't take me. I'm too little, that I am," said the billy-goat; "wait a bit till the second bushy billy-goat comes; he's much bigger."

"Then scamper," said the troll.

A little while after came the second bushy billy-goat and wanted to cross the bridge.

"TRIP, TRAP! TRIP, TRAP! TRIP, TRAP!" went the bridge.

"WHO'S THAT tripping over my bridge?" roared the troll.

"Oh, it's the second bushy billy-goat who is going to the mountains to get fat," said the billy-goat, who hadn't quite such a small voice.

"Now, I'm coming for you," said the troll.

"Oh, no, don't take me; wait a little till the big bushy billy-goat comes; he's much, much bigger."

"Scamper then," said the troll.

In a little while up came the big Bushy billy-goat.

"TRIP, TRAP! TRIP, TRAP! TRIP, TRAP!" went the bridge, for the billy-goat was so heavy that the bridge creaked and groaned under him.

"WHO'S THAT tramping over my bridge?" roared the troll.

"IT IS THE BIG BUSHY BILLY-GOAT," said the billy-goat, who had a very deep and very gruff voice.

"Now, I'm coming for you," roared the troll.

> Yes, come on! Of spears I have two
> With those I am going to go for you.
> I have also got two rubble-stones,
> With those I'll crush your marrow and bones.

That was what the billy-goat said.

And so he flew at the troll and poked his eyes out with his horns, cracked his bones, and crushed him to pieces and tossed him down the waterfall, and then he went up to his mountain pasture. There the bushy billy-goats got so fat they were scarce able to walk home again; and if the fat hasn't fallen off them, why, they're still fat, on the edge of bursting their hides.

> And snip, snap, snout,
> And now this tale is out.

Tatterhood

ONCE on a time there were a king and a queen who had no children, and that gave the queen much grief. She scarce had one happy hour. She was always bewailing and bemoaning herself, and saying how dull and lonesome it was in the palace.

"If we had children there'd be life enough," she said.

Wherever she went in all her realm she found God's blessing in children, even in the vilest hut; and wherever she came she heard the wives scolding the children, and saying how they had done that and that wrong. And this the queen thought very nice and this she wanted to do herself. At last the king and queen took into their palace a strange little girl to rear up, that they might have her always with them. They were to bring her up and scold her as if she were their own child.

One day the little maid whom they had taken as their own was running around in the palace yard, playing with a golden apple. Just then an old beggar wife, who had a little girl with her, came by, and it wasn't long before the little maid and the beggar's child were friends and began to play together, and to toss the golden apple about between them. The queen, who was sitting at her window, saw this and she tapped on the pane for her foster-daughter to come up. She went at once, but the beggar girl went up too; and as they went into the queen's bower, each held the other by the hand. Then the queen began to scold the little lady.

"It is not for you to run and play with a tattered beggar's brat," she said.

And so she wanted to chase away the lassie.

"If the queen only knew my mother's power, she'd not chase me away," said the little lassie; and when the queen asked her to say more plainly what she meant, she told her how her mother could get her children if she chose. The queen wouldn't believe it, but the lassie held her own and said every word of it was true, and bade the queen only to try and make her mother do it. So the queen sent the lassie down to fetch up her mother.

"Do you know what your daughter says?" asked the queen of the beggar woman, as soon as she came into the room.

No, the beggar wife knew nothing about it.

"She says you can get me children if you will," said the queen.

"Queens shouldn't listen to beggar brats' stories," said the beggar woman, and strode out of the room.

Then the queen got angry, and wanted again to chase away the little lassie; but she declared it was true every word that she had said.

"Let the queen only give my mother a drop to drink," said the lassie; "when she gets merry she'll soon find out a way to help you."

The queen was ready to try this, so the beggar wife was fetched up again, and treated both with wine and mead as much as she chose; and so it was not long before her tongue began to wag. Then the queen came out again with the same question she had asked before.

"One way to help you perhaps I know," said the beggar wife. "The queen must make them bring in two pails of water some evening before she goes to bed. In each of them she must wash herself, and afterwards throw away the water under the bed. When she looks under the bed the next morning, two flowers will have sprung up, one fair and one ugly. The fair one she must eat, the ugly one she must let stand; but mind she doesn't forget the last." That was what the beggar wife said.

Yes, the queen did what the beggar wife advised her to do. She had the water brought up in two pails, washed herself in them, and emptied them under the bed. And lo! when she looked under the bed next morning, there stood two flowers; one was ugly and foul and had black leaves, but the other was so bright and fair and lovely she had never seen its like.

So she ate it up at once. But the pretty flower tasted so sweet that she couldn't help herself. She ate the other up too, for she thought: "It can't hurt or help one much either way, I'll be bound."

Well, sure enough, after a while the queen was brought to bed. First she had a girl who had a wooden spoon in her hand and rode upon a billy-goat. Loathly and ugly she was, and the very moment she came into the world she bawled out: "Mamma."

"If I'm your mamma," said the queen, "God give me grace to mend my ways."

"Oh, don't be sorry," said the girl, who rode on the goat, "for one will soon come after me who is better looking."

So, after a while, the queen had another girl, who was so fair and sweet no one had ever set eyes on such a lovely child, and with her you may fancy the queen was very well pleased. The elder twin they called Tatterhood, because she was always so ugly and ragged, and because she had a hood which hung about her ears in tatters. The queen could scarce bear to look at her, and the maids tried to shut her up in a room by herself, but it was all no good; where the younger twin was, there she must also be, and no one could ever keep them apart.

Well, one Christmas Eve, when they were half grown up, there rose such a frightful noise and clatter in the gallery outside the queen's bower. Tatterhood asked what it was that dashed and crashed so out on the gallery.

"Oh," said the queen, "it isn't worth asking about."

But Tatterhood wouldn't give over till she found out what it was, and so the queen told her it was a pack of trolls and witches who had come there to keep Christmas. Tatterhood said she'd go out and drive them away, and in spite of all they could say and however much they begged and prayed her to let the trolls alone, she must and would go out to drive the witches off. But she begged the queen to mind and keep all the doors close shut, so that not one of them came so much as the least bit ajar. Having said this, off she went with her wooden spoon, and began to hunt and sweep away the hags; and all this while there was such a pother out in the gallery, the like of it was never heard. The whole palace creaked and groaned as if every joint and beam were going to be torn out of its place. Somehow or other one of the doors did get the least bit ajar. Then her twin sister just peeped out to see how things were going with Tatterhood, and put her head a tiny bit through the opening. But, POP! up came an old witch, and whipped off her head, and stuck a calf's head on her shoulders instead; and so the princess ran back into the room on all fours and began to moo like a calf. When Tatterhood came back and saw her sister, she scolded them all round, and was very angry because they hadn't kept better watch, and asked them what they thought of their heedlessness now, when her sister was turned into a calf.

"But still I'll see if I can't set her free," she said.

Then she asked the king for a ship in full trim, and well fitted with stores; but captain and sailors she wouldn't have. No, she would sail away with her sister all alone, and as there was no holding her back, at last they let her have her own way.

Then Tatterhood sailed off, and steered her ship right under the land where the witches dwelt, and when she came to the landing-place she told her sister to stay quite still on board the ship; but she herself rode on her billy-goat up to the witches' castle. When she got there, one of the windows was open, and there she saw her sister's head standing on the windowsill; so she galloped her goat into the courtyard, snapped up the head, and set off with it. After her came the witches to try to get the head again, and they flocked about her as thick as a swarm of bees or a nest of ants; but the billy-goat snorted and puffed and butted with his horns, and Tatterhood beat and banged them about with her wooden spoon; and so the pack of witches had to give it up. So Tatterhood got back to her ship, took the calf's head off her sister, and put her own on again, and then her sister was a beautiful maiden as she had been before. After that she sailed a long, long way to the realm of a strange king.

The king of that land was a widower, and had an only son. When he saw the strange sail, he sent messengers down to the strand to find out whence it came, and who owned it; but when the king's men came down there, they saw never a living soul on board but Tatterhood, and there she was, riding round and round the deck on her billy-goat at full speed, so her straggling hair flew about her head. The folk from the palace were all amazed at this sight, and asked, were there not more on board? Yes, there were; she had a sister with her, said Tatterhood. Her, too, they wanted to see, but Tatterhood said no.

"No one shall see her unless the king comes himself," she said, and so she began to gallop about on her billy-goat till the deck thundered again.

When the servants got back to the palace and told what they had seen and heard down at the ship, the king was for setting out at once, that he might see the lassie who rode on the billy-goat. When he got there, Tatterhood led out her sister, and she was so fair and gentle the king fell over head and ears in love with her as he stood. He brought them both back with him to the palace, and wanted to have the sister for his queen. But Tatterhood said no, the king couldn't have her in any way, unless the king's son chose to have Tatterhood. That you may fancy the prince was very loath to do, such an ugly hussy as Tatterhood was; but at last the king and all the others in the palace talked him over, and he yielded, giving his word to take her for his queen; but he didn't like it much and he moped about.

Now they set about the wedding, with both brewing and baking, and when all was ready, they were to go to church. But the prince thought it the weariest churching he had ever had in all his life. First the king drove off with his bride, and she was so lovely and so grand all the people stopped to look after her all along the road, and they stared at her till she was out of sight. After them came the prince on horseback by the side of Tatterhood, who trotted along on her billy-goat with her wooden spoon in her fist, and to look at him, it was more like going to a burial than a wedding, and that his own, so sorrowful he seemed, and with never a word to say.

Tatterhood

"Why don't you talk?" asked Tatterhood, when they had ridden a bit.

"What should I talk about?" answered the prince.

"You might ask me why I ride upon this ugly billy-goat," said Tatterhood.

"Why do you ride on that ugly billy-goat?" asked the prince.

"Is that an ugly billy-goat? Why, it's the grandest horse bride ever rode on," answered Tatterhood; and in a trice the billy-goat became a horse, and that the finest the prince had ever set eyes on.

Then they rode on again a bit, but the prince was just as woeful as before, and couldn't get a word out. So Tatterhood asked him again why he didn't talk, and when the prince answered he didn't know what to talk about, she said:

"You can ask me why I ride with this ugly spoon in my fist."

"Why do you ride with that ugly spoon?" asked the prince.

"Is that an ugly spoon? Why, it's the loveliest silver wand bride ever bore," said Tatterhood; and in a trice it became a silver wand, so dazzling bright, the sunbeams glistened from it.

So they rode on another bit, but the prince was just as sorrowful, and said never a word. In a little while, Tatterhood asked him again why he didn't talk, and bade him ask why she wore that ugly grey hood on her head.

"Why do you wear that ugly grey hood on your head?" asked the prince.

"Is that an ugly hood? Why, it's the brightest golden crown bride ever wore," answered Tatterhood, and it became a crown on the spot.

Now they rode on a long while again, and the prince was so woeful that he sat without sound or speech just as before. So his bride asked him again why he didn't talk, and bade him ask now, why her face was so ugly and ashen grey.

"Yes, why is your face so ugly and ashen grey?" asked the prince.

"I ugly?" said the bride. "You think my sister pretty, but I am ten times prettier." And lo! when the prince looked at her, she was so lovely, he thought there never was so lovely a maiden in all the world. And then you can be sure the prince found his tongue, and no longer rode along hanging down his head.

So they drank the bridal cup both deep and long, and after that both prince and king set out with their brides to the princesses' father's palace, and there they had another bridal feast, and drank anew, both deep and long. There was no end to the fun; and, if you make haste and run to the king's palace, there may perhaps still be a drop of the bridal ale left for you.

Dapplegrim

ONCE on a time there was a rich couple who had twelve sons; but the youngest, when he was grown up, said he wouldn't stay any longer at home, but be off into the world to try his luck. His father and mother said he did very well at home and had better stay where he was. But no, he couldn't rest; he would set off and he must set off. So at last they had to let him go. When he had walked a good bit, he came to the king's farms. There he asked for a place, and that he got.

Now the daughter of the king of that land had been carried off into the mountain by a troll, and the king had no other children; so he and all his land were in great grief and sorrow, and the king gave his word that anyone who could set her free should have the princess and half the kingdom. But there was no one who could do it, though many tried.

So when the lad had been there a year or so, he longed to go home again and see his father and mother, and back he went. But when he got home, his father and mother were dead, and his brothers had shared all that the old people owned between them and there was nothing left for the lad.

"Shan't I have anything at all, then, out of Father's and Mother's goods?" said the lad.

"Who could tell you were still alive, when you went gadding and wandering about so long?" said his brothers. "But all the same, there are twelve mares up on the hill which we haven't yet shared among us. If you choose to take them for your share, you're quite welcome."

Yes, the lad was quite content; so he thanked his brothers and went at once up to the hill where the twelve mares were out at grass. When he got up there and found them, each of them had a foal at her side; and one of them had besides, along with her, a big dapple-grey foal that was so sleek that the sun shone from its coat.

"You are handsome, you, my little foal," said the lad.

"Yes," said the foal, "but if you'll kill all the other foals, so that I may run and suck all the mares for a year you'll see how big and handsome I'll be then."

Yes, the lad was ready to do that; so he killed all the twelve foals and went home again.

When he came back the next year to look after his foal and mares, the foal was so fat and sleek that the sun shone from its coat, and it had grown so big the lad had hard work to mount it. As for the mares, they had each of them another foal.

"Well, it's quite plain I lost nothing by letting you suck all my twelve mares," said the lad to the yearling, "but now you're big enough to come along with me."

"No," said the colt, "I must bide here a year longer. And now kill all the twelve foals, that I may suck all the mares this year too, and you'll see how big and handsome I'll be by summer."

Yes, the lad did that; and next year when he went up to the hill to look after his colt and the mares, each mare had her foal. But the dapple colt was so tall the lad couldn't reach up to his crest when he wanted to feel how fat he was, and so sleek he was, too, that his coat glistened in the sunshine.

"Big and beautiful you were last year, my colt," said the lad, "but this year you're far grander. There's no such horse in the king's stable. But now you must come along with me."

"No," said Dapple again. "I must stay here one year more. Kill the twelve foals as before, that I may suck the mares this year too; then you'll see how I look next summer."

Yes, the lad did that. He killed the foals and went away home.

But when he went up next year to look after Dapple and the mares, he was quite astonished. So tall and stout and sturdy he never thought a horse could be; for Dapple had to lie down on all fours before the lad could mount him, and it was hard work to get up even then, although he lay flat. And his coat was so smooth and sleek, the sunbeams shone from it as from a looking-glass.

This time Dapple was willing to follow the lad, so he jumped up on his back, and when he came riding home to his brothers, they all clapped their hands and crossed themselves, for such a horse they had never heard of nor seen before.

"If you will get me the best shoes you can for my horse, and the grandest saddle and bridle that are to be found," said the lad, "you may have my twelve mares that graze up on the hill yonder, and their twelve foals into the bargain." For you must know that this year, too, every mare had her foal.

Yes, his brothers were ready to do that, and so the lad got such strong shoes under his horse that the stones flew high aloft as he rode away across the hills; and he had a golden saddle and a golden bridle that gleamed and glistened a long way off.

"Now we're off to the king's farms," said Dapplegrim—that was his name, "but mind you ask the king for plenty of room in the stable and good fodder for me."

Yes, the lad said he would mind, he'd be sure not to forget. So he rode off and you may be sure it wasn't long, on a horse like that, before he got to the king's farms.

When he came there, the king was standing on the steps, and stared and stared at the man who came riding along.

"Nay, nay!" said he. "Such a man and such a horse I never yet saw in all my life."

And when the lad asked if he could get a place in the king's household, the king was so glad he was ready to jump and dance as he stood on the steps.

One thing was sure and certain, and that was that the king had use for such a man.

"Aye," said the lad, "but I must have good stable-room for my horse, and fodder that one can trust."

Dapplegrim

Yes, he should have meadow-hay and oats, as much as Dapple could cram, and all the other knights had to lead their horses out of the stable that Dapplegrim might stand alone and have it all to himself.

But it wasn't long before all the others in the king's household began to be jealous of the lad, and there was no end to the bad things they would have done to him, if they had only dared. At last they thought of telling the king he had said he was man enough to set free the king's daughter—whom the troll had long since carried away into the mountain—if he only chose. The king called the lad before him, and said he had heard the lad said he was good to do this and that, and now he must do it. If he did it, he knew how the king had promised his daughter and half the kingdom, and that promise would be faithfully kept; if he didn't, he should be killed.

The lad kept on saying he had never said any such thing, but it was no good—the king wouldn't listen with that ear. And so the end of it was he was forced to say he'd go and try.

So he went into the stable, and sad and heavy-hearted he was. And then Dapplegrim asked him why he was so sad.

The lad told him all that had happened, and said he couldn't tell which way to turn.

"For, as for setting the princess free, that certainly can't be done," said the lad.

"Oh, but it might be done, perhaps," said Dapplegrim. "I'll help you through; but you must first have me well shod. You must go and ask for twenty pounds of iron and twelve pounds of steel for the shoes, and one smith to hammer and another to hold."

Yes, the lad did that, and he didn't get no for an answer. He got both the iron and the steel and the smiths, and so Dapplegrim was shod both strong and well, and off rode the lad from the courtyard in a cloud of dust.

But when he came to the mountain into which the princess had been carried, the pinch was how to get up the mountain wall and reach the place where he could enter the troll's abode. For the mountain stood straight up and down right on end, as upright as a house wall and as slippery as a windowpane.

The first time the lad went at it he got a little way up; but then Dapple's fore-legs slipped and down they went again, with a sound like thunder on the hill.

The second time he rode at it he got some way further up; but then one fore-leg slipped and down they went, with a crash like a landslide.

But the third time Dapplegrim said:

"Now we must show our mettle!" and went at it again till the stones flew heaven high about them, and so they got up.

Then the lad rode right into the mountain at full speed, and caught up the princess and threw her over his saddle-bow and out and down again before the troll had time even to get on his legs. And so the princess was freed.

When the lad came back to the court, the king was both happy and glad to get his daughter back, that you may well believe. But somehow or other, though I don't know how, the others about the court had so brought it about that the king was angry with the lad after all.

"Thanks you shall have for freeing my daughter," said he to the lad, when he brought the princess into the hall. And then the king wanted him to go away.

"She ought to be mine as well as yours, for you're a word-fast man, I hope," said the lad.

"Oh, yes, oh, yes," said the king, "have her you shall, since I said it. But first of all, you must make the sun shine into my hall." Now you must know there was a high, steep ridge of rock close outside the windows, which kept all the sunshine away.

"That wasn't in our bargain," answered the lad; "but I see this is past praying against. I'll have to go and try my best, for the princess I must and will have."

So down he went to Dapple and told him what the king wanted now, and Dapplegrim thought it might perhaps be done. But first he must be new shod; and for that twenty pounds of iron and twelve pounds of steel were needed, and two smiths, one to hammer and the other to hold. And then they'd soon get the sun to shine into the king's hall.

So when the lad asked for all these things, he got them at once—the king couldn't say nay, for very shame. And so Dapplegrim got new shoes, and such shoes! Then the lad jumped upon his back and off they went again; and for every leap that Dapplegrim gave, down sank the ridge fifteen ells into the earth, and so they went on till there was nothing left of the ridge for the king to see.

When the lad got back to the court, he asked the king if the princess were not his own, for now no one could say that the sun didn't shine into the hall. But the others had set the king up again; and so he answered the lad should have her of course, he had never thought of anything else, but first he must get as grand a horse for the bride to ride on to church as the bridegroom had himself.

The lad said the king hadn't spoken a word about this before, and that he thought he had now fairly earned the princess; but the king held to his own and more. If the lad couldn't do that, he should lose his life, said the king. The lad went down to the stable, and sad and down-hearted he was, you may be sure. And there he told Dapplegrim all about it: how the king had laid that task on him, to find the bride as good a horse as the bridegroom had himself, else he would lose his life.

"But that's not so easy," he said, "for your match isn't to be found in the wide world."

"Oh, yes. I have a match," said Dapplegrim; "but 'tisn't so easy to find him, for he lives in Hell. Still we'll try. Now you must go up to the king and ask for new shoes for me: twenty pounds of iron and twelve pounds of steel, and two smiths, one to hammer and one to hold; and mind you see that the points and ends of these shoes are sharp. And twelve sacks of rye, and twelve sacks of barley, and twelve slaughtered oxen, we must have with us; and mind, we must have the twelve ox-hides, with twelve hundred spikes driven into each. And, let me see, a big tar-barrel so big that it takes twelve barrels of tar to fill it. All this we need."

So the lad went up to the king and asked for all that Dapplegrim had said, and the king again thought he couldn't say nay, for shame's sake, and so the lad got all he wanted.

Well, he jumped up on Dapplegrim's back and rode away off, and when he had ridden far, far over hills and mountains, Dapplegrim asked:

"Do you hear anything?"

"Yes, I hear an awful hissing and rustling up in the air," said the lad. "I think I'm getting afraid."

"That's all the wild birds that fly through the wood. They are sent to stop us. But just cut a hole in the grain-sacks, and then they'll have so much to do with the grain, they'll forget us quite."

Yes, the lad did that; he cut holes in the grain-sacks, so that the rye and barley ran out on all sides. Then all the wild birds that were in the wood came flying round them so thick that the sunbeams grew dark. But as soon as they saw the grain, they couldn't keep to their purpose, but flew down and began to pick and scratch at the rye and barley; and after that they began to fight among themselves. As for Dapplegrim and the lad, they forgot all about them, and did them no harm.

So the lad rode on and on—far, far over mountains and valleys and hills and plains. Then Dapplegrim began to prick up his ears again, and at last he asked the lad if he heard anything.

"Yes, now I hear such an ugly roaring and howling in the wood all round, it makes me quite afraid."

"Ah!" said Dapplegrim. "That's all the wild beasts that range through the wood, and they're sent out to stop us. But just cast out the carcasses of the twelve oxen, that will give them enough to do, and so they'll forget us outright."

Yes, the lad cast out the carcasses, and then came all the wild beasts in the wood, bears and wolves and lions—all kinds of ferocious beasts. But when they saw the meat, they began to fight for it among themselves till blood flowed in streams; and Dapplegrim and the lad they quite forgot.

Dapplegrim

So the lad rode far away across many, many blue mountains, for Dapplegrim didn't let the grass grow under him, you may believe. At last Dapple gave a great neigh.

"Do you hear anything?" he said.

"Yes, I hear something like a colt neighing faintly, far, far away," answered the lad.

"That's a full-grown colt," said Dapplegrim. "It only sounds so faint because he is so far, far away."

After that they travelled a good bit, across another blue mountain and still a little bit further. Then Dapplegrim gave another neigh.

"Do you hear anything now?" he said.

"Yes, now I hear a neigh like a full-grown horse," answered the lad.

"Aye! Aye!" said Dapplegrim. "You'll soon hear him again, and then you'll hear what a voice he's got."

They travelled over still another blue mountain and even a little bit further. Then Dapplegrim neighed the third time; but before he could ask the lad if he heard anything, something gave such a neigh across the heathery hillside, the lad thought hill and rock would surely be rent asunder.

"Now he's here!" said Dapplegrim. "Make haste now, and throw the ox-hides with the spikes in them over me, and throw down the tar-barrel on the ground; then climb up into that great spruce-fir yonder. When it comes, fire will flash out of both nostrils, and then the tar-barrel will catch fire. Now watch well. If the flame rises, I win; if it falls, I lose. But if you see me winning, take and cast the bridle—you must take it off me—over its head, and then it will be tame."

So just as the lad had done throwing the ox-hides with the spikes over Dapplegrim, and had cast down the tar-barrel on the ground, and had got well up into the spruce-fir, up galloped a horse, with fire flashing out of his nostrils, and the flame caught the tar-barrel at once. Then Dapplegrim and the strange horse began to fight till the stones flew sky high. They bit and they kicked, with both fore-feet and hind-feet, and some of the time the lad watched the fight and some of the time he watched the tar-barrel; but by and by the flame began to rise, for wherever the strange horse kicked or bit he met the spiked hides; and at last he had to yield. When the lad saw that, he wasn't long in getting down from the tree and throwing the bridle over its head, and then it was so tame you could hold it with a pack-thread.

And what do you think? That horse was dappled too, and looked so much like Dapplegrim you couldn't tell which was which. Then the lad jumped up on the new Dapple he had broken and rode home to the king's court again, and Dapplegrim ran loose by his side. So when he got home, there stood the king out in the yard.

"Can you tell me now," said the lad, "which is the horse I have caught and broken, and which is the one I had before? If you can't, I think your daughter is fairly mine."

The king went and looked at both Dapples, high and low, before and behind, but there wasn't a hair on one which wasn't on the other as well. "No," said the king, "that I can't. And since you've got my daughter such a grand horse for her wedding, you shall have her with all my heart. But still, we'll have one trial more, just to see whether you're fated to have her. First she shall hide herself twice, and then you shall hide yourself twice. If you can find out her hiding place, and she can't find out yours, why, then you're fated to have her, and so you shall have her."

"That's not in the bargain either," said the lad; "but we must just try, since it must be so." And so the princess went off to hide herself first.

She turned herself into a duck, and lay swimming on a pond that was close to the hall. But the lad only ran down to the stable and asked Dapplegrim what she had done with herself.

"Oh, you only need to take your gun," said Dapplegrim, "and go down to the brink of the pond and aim at the duck which lies swimming about there, and she'll soon show herself."

The lad snatched up his gun and ran off to the pond. "I'll just take a pop at this duck," he said, and began to aim at it.

Dapplegrim

"Oh, no, dear me, don't shoot!" said the princess.

And so he had found her that time.

The second time the princess turned herself into a loaf of bread and laid herself on the table among four other loaves, and so like was she to the others, no one could say which was which.

But the lad went again down to the stable to Dapplegrim, and said how the princess had hidden herself again, and he couldn't tell at all what had become of her.

"Oh, just take and sharpen a good bread-knife," said Dapplegrim, "and do as if you were going to cut in two the third loaf on the left hand of those four loaves which are lying on the table in the king's kitchen, and you'll find her soon enough."

Yes, down went the lad to the kitchen, and began to sharpen the biggest bread-knife he could lay hands on; then he caught hold of the third loaf on the left hand, and put the knife to it as though he were going to cut it in two.

"Oh, no, dear me. Don't cut. It is I," said the princess.

So he had found her this time too.

Then he was to go and hide; but he and Dapplegrim had settled it all so well beforehand, it wasn't easy to find him. First he turned himself into a tick and hid himself in Dapplegrim's left nostril. And the princess went about hunting him everywhere, high and low. At last she wanted to go into Dapplegrim's stall, but he began to bite and kick so that she dared not go near him, and so she couldn't find the lad.

"Well," she said, "since I can't find you, you must show where you are yourself." And in a trice the lad stood there on the stable floor.

The second time Dapplegrim told him again what to do; and then he turned himself into a clod of earth and stuck himself between Dapple's hoof and shoe on the near fore-foot. The princess went about looking and hunting. At last she came into the stable and wanted to go into Dapplegrim's stall. This time he let her come up to him, and she pried high and low. But under his hoofs she couldn't get, he stood too firmly on his feet for that, and so she couldn't find the lad.

168

Dapplegrim

"Well, you must just show yourself, for I'm sure I can't find you," said the princess, and as she spoke the lad stood by her side on the stable floor.

"Now you are mine indeed," said the lad to the princess; "for now you can see I'm fated to have her," he said to the king.

"Yes, if it is so fated, it must so be," said the king.

Then they got ready the wedding in downright earnest, and lost no time about it. And the lad got on Dapplegrim and the princess on Dapplegrim's match, and then you may be sure they were not long on their way to the church.

Gudbrand on the Hillside

ONCE on a time there was a man whose name was Gudbrand. He had a farm which lay far, far away upon a hillside, and so they called him Gudbrand on the Hillside.

He and his wife lived so happily together and agreed so well about everything, that all the husband did the wife thought so well done it couldn't be done any better, and she was always glad whatever he turned his hand to. The farm was their own land, and they had a hundred dollars lying at the bottom of their chest, and two cows tethered up in a stall in their farmyard.

Then one day his wife said to Gudbrand:

"I think we ought to take one of our cows into town and sell it; for then we shall have some money in hand, and such well-to-do people as we ought to have ready money like the rest of the world. As for the hundred dollars at the bottom of the chest, we can't make a hole in them, and I'm sure I don't know what we want with more than one cow. Besides, we shall gain a little in another way; for then I shall get off with only looking after one cow, instead of having, as now, to feed and litter and water two."

Well, Gudbrand thought his wife talked right good sense, so he set off at once with the cow on his way to town to sell her; but when he got to town, there was no one who would buy his cow.

"Well," thought Gudbrand, "then I can go home again with my cow. I've both stable and tether for her, that I know, and the road is no farther out than in." And with that he began to toddle home with his cow.

But when he had gone a bit of the way, he met a man who had a horse to sell, so Gudbrand thought 'twas better to have a horse than a cow, so he swapped with the man. A little farther on he met a man walking along and driving a fat pig before him, and he thought it better to have a fat pig than a horse, so he swapped with the man. After that he went a little farther, and then he met a man with a goat; so he thought it was surely better to have a goat than a pig, and so he swapped with the man who owned the goat. Then he went on a good bit till he met a man who had a sheep, and he swapped with him too, for he thought it always better to have a sheep than a goat. After a while he met a man with a goose, and he swapped away the sheep for the goose. And when he had walked a long, long time, he met a man with a cock, and he swapped with him, for he thought in this wise: " 'Tis surely better to have a cock than a goose." Then he went on till the day was far spent, and he began to get very hungry, so he sold the cock for a shilling, and bought food with the money, for, thought Gudbrand on the Hillside: " 'Tis always better to save one's life than to have a cock."

After that he went on home till he reached his nearest neighbour's house, where he turned in.

"Well," said the owner of the house, "how did things go with you in town?"

"Rather so so," said Gudbrand. "I can't praise my luck, nor do I blame it either," and with that he told the whole story from first to last.

"Ah," said his friend, "you'll get nicely called over the coals, that one can see, when you get home to your wife. Heaven help you, I wouldn't stand in your shoes for anything."

"Well," said Gudbrand on the Hillside, "I think things might have gone much worse with me; but now, whether I have done wrong or not, I have so kind a goodwife she never has a word to say against anything that I do."

"Oh!" answered his neighbour. "I hear what you say, but I don't believe it for all that."

"Shall we lay a bet on it?" asked Gudbrand on the Hillside. "I have a hundred dollars at the bottom of my chest at home; will you lay as many against them?"

Yes, the friend was ready to bet; so Gudbrand stayed there till evening, when it began to get dark; and then they went together to his house, and the neighbour was to stand outside the door and listen, while Gudbrand himself went in to see his wife.

"Good evening!" said Gudbrand on the Hillside, when he came in.

"Good evening, good evening! Oh, praise to God, is that you?" said his wife.

Yes, so it was! Then the wife asked how things had gone with him in town.

"Oh, only so so," answered Gudbrand, "not much to brag of. When I got to the town, there was no one who would buy the cow, so I swapped it away for a horse."

"For a horse?" said his wife. "Well, for that you really shall have many thanks," said the wife. "We are so well to do that we may drive to church, just as well as other people; and if we choose to keep a horse we have a right to get one, I should think. Go out and put the horse in the stable, children."

"Well," said Gudbrand, "but I just don't have the horse after all, for when I got a bit farther on the road, I swapped it away for a pig."

"Oh, no, really!" cried the wife. "You did just as I should have done myself. A thousand thanks! Now we can have ham in the house and something to offer people when they come to see us, we two. What do we want with a horse? People would only say we had got so proud that we couldn't walk to church as we have always been doing. Run out, children, and put up the pig in the sty."

"But I've not got the pig either," said Gudbrand, "for when I got a little farther on, I swapped it away for a milch goat."

"Bless us," cried his wife, "how well you manage everything! Now I think it over, what should I do with a pig? People would only point at us and say: 'Yonder they eat up all they have got.' No! Now I have got a goat, and I shall have milk and cheese, and keep the goat too. Let in the goat, children."

"Nay, but I haven't got the goat either," said Gudbrand, "for a little farther on I swapped it away, and got a fine sheep instead."

"You don't say so!" cried his wife. "Why, you do everything to please me, just as if I had been with you. What do we want with a goat? If I had it, I should lose half my time in climbing up the mountains and hills to get it down again at night. No, if I have a sheep, I shall have both wool and clothing, and fresh meat in the house. Run out, let in the sheep, children."

"But I haven't got the sheep any more than the rest," said Gudbrand, "for when I had gone a bit farther, I swapped it away for a goose."

"Thank you for that," cried his wife, "and many thanks too! What should I do with a sheep? I have neither spinning wheel, nor loom; nor should I care to worry myself with cutting and shaping and sewing clothes. We can buy clothes now, as we have always done; and now I shall have roast goose, which I have longed for so often; and, besides, there's down to stuff my little pillow with. Run out and let in the goose, children."

"Well," said Gudbrand, "but I haven't the goose either; for when I had gone a bit farther, I swapped it away for a cock."

"Dear me," cried his wife, "how you think of everything! Just as I should have done myself. A cock! Think of that! Why it's as good as an eight-day clock; for every morning the cock crows at four o'clock, and we shall be able to stir our stumps in good time. What should we do with a goose? I don't know how to cook it, and as for my pillow, I can stuff it with sedge-grass. Run out and let in the cock, children."

"But after all, I haven't got the cock either," said Gudbrand, "for when I had gone a bit farther, I got as hungry as a wolf; so I was forced to sell the cock for a shilling, to save my life."

"Now, God be praised that you did so!" cried his wife. "Whatever you do, you do it always just after my own heart. What should we do with the cock? We are our own masters, I should think, and can lie a-bed in the morning as long as we like. Heaven be thanked that I have got you safe back again. You who do everything so well that I want neither cock nor goose, neither pigs nor cows."

Then Gudbrand opened the door.

"Have I won the hundred dollars now?" he said, and his neighbour was forced to allow that he had.

The Hen Trips in the Mountain

ONCE on a time there was an old widow who lived far away from the rest of the world, up under a hillside, with her three daughters. She was so poor that she owned nothing but one single hen, which she prized as the apple of her eye. She cackled to it and she cared for it both early and late. But one day, all at once, the hen was missing. The old wife went out and round and round the cottage, cackling and calling for her hen; but it was gone, and there was no getting it back.

So the woman said to her eldest daughter: "You must just go out and see if you can find our hen, for have it back we must, even if we have to fetch it out of the mountain."

Yes, the daughter was ready to go, and she set off and walked up and down, and looked and called, but no hen could she find. But all at once, just as she was about to give up the hunt, she heard someone calling out from the mountainside:

> The hen trips in the mountain!
> The hen trips in the mountain!

So she went to see what it was. But over at the mountainside she fell through a trap-door, deep, deep down into a vault under ground. Down there she walked through many rooms, each finer than the other; but in the innermost room of all, a great ugly mountain troll came up to her.

"Will you be my sweetheart?" he said.

"No! No!" she said, that she wouldn't at all. All she wanted was to get above ground again and to look for her hen which was lost. Then the troll got so angry that he took her up and wrung her head off, and threw both head and trunk down into the cellar.

The Hen Trips in the Mountain

Her mother was sitting at home waiting and waiting, but no daughter came. So after she had waited a bit longer, and neither heard nor saw anything of her daughter, she said to her midmost daughter that she must go out and look for her sister, and she added:

"You can just give our hen a call at the same time."

Then the second sister set off, and the very same thing befell her; she went about looking and calling, and all at once she too heard a voice calling out from the mountainside:

> The hen trips in the mountain!
> The hen trips in the mountain!

She thought this strange, and went to see what it could be; and so she too fell through the trap-door, deep, deep down into the vault. There she went from room to room, and in the innermost one the mountain troll came to her and asked if she would be his sweetheart. No, that she wouldn't! All she wanted was to get above ground again, and hunt for her hen which was lost. So the troll got angry, and took her up and wrung her head off, and threw both head and trunk down into the cellar.

Now, when the old woman had sat and waited seven lengths and seven breadths for her second daughter, and could neither see nor hear anything of her, she said to the youngest:

"Now, you really must set off and look for your sisters. 'Twas bad to lose the hen, but 'twill be worse still if we lose both your sisters; and you can give the hen a call at the same time."

Yes, the youngest was ready to go; so she walked up and down, hunting for her sisters and calling the hen, but she could neither see nor hear anything of them. So at long last she too came up to the mountain and heard how something said:

> The hen trips in the mountain!
> The hen trips in the mountain!

She thought this strange, so she too went to see what it was, and fell through the trap-door deep, deep down into a vault. Down there she

176

went from one room to another, each grander than the other; but she wasn't at all afraid, and took good time to look about her. So, as she was peeping into this and that, she caught sight of the trap-door into the cellar too, and looked down it, and what should she see there but her sisters, who lay dead. As soon as she had got the trap-door to the cellar well closed, the mountain troll came to her.

"Will you be my sweetheart?" he asked.

"With all my heart," answered the girl, for she saw very well how it had gone with her sisters. When the troll heard that, he got her beautiful clothes, the finest she ever could wish; and everything else she wanted she got, so glad was he that anyone would be his sweetheart.

But when she had been there a little while, she was one day even more doleful and downcast than was her wont. So the troll asked her what was the matter, and why she was so sad.

"Oh," said the girl, "it's because I can't get home to my mother. She's hard pinched, I know, for meat and drink and has no one with her."

"Well," said the troll, "I can't let you go to see her; but just stuff some food into a sack, and I'll carry it to her."

Yes, she would do so! she said, with many thanks; but at the bottom of the sack she stuffed a lot of gold and silver, and afterwards she laid a little food on the top of the gold and silver. Then she told the troll the sack was ready, but he must be sure not to look into it. So he gave his word he wouldn't, and set off. Now as the troll walked off, she peeped out after him through a chink in the trap-door; but when he had gone a bit on the way, he said:

"This sack is so heavy, I'll just see what there is inside it." He was about to untie the mouth of the sack, when the girl called:

"I see you! I see you!"

"The deuce you do!" said the troll. "You have plaguy sharp eyes in your head."

So he threw the sack over his shoulder, and dared not try to look into it again. When he reached the widow's cottage, he threw the sack in through the door.

The Hen Trips in the Mountain

"Here you have food from your daughter; she doesn't want for anything," he said.

When the girl had been in the mountain a good bit longer, one day a billy-goat fell down the trap-door.

"Who sent for you, I should like to know, you long-bearded beast!" said the troll, who was in an awful rage, and with that he whipped up the goat, and wrung his head off, and threw him down into the cellar.

"Oh," said the girl, "why did you do that? I might have had the goat to play with down here."

"Well," said the troll, "you needn't be so down in the mouth about it, I should think, for I can soon put life into the billy-goat again."

So saying, he took a flask which hung up against the wall, put the billy-goat's head on his body again, and smeared it with some ointment out of the flask, and he was as well and as lively as ever.

"Ho-ho!" said the girl to herself. "That flask is worth something—that it is."

So when she had been some time longer in the mountain, she watched for a day when the troll was away, took her eldest sister, and, putting her head on her shoulders, smeared her with some of the ointment out of the flask, just as she had seen the troll do with the billy-goat. And in a trice her sister came to life again. Then the girl stuffed her into a sack, laid a little food over her, and, as soon as the troll came home, she said to him:

"Oh, please; oh, dear! Now do go home to my mother with a morsel of food again, poor thing! She's both hungry and thirsty, I'll be bound; and besides that, she's all alone in the world. But you must mind and not look into the sack."

Well, he said, he would carry the sack; and he said, too, that he would not look into it; but when he had gone a little way, he thought the sack got awfully heavy; and when he had gone a bit farther he said to himself:

"Come what will, I must see what's inside this sack, for however sharp her eyes may be, she can't see me now."

The Hen Trips in the Mountain

But just as he was about to untie the sack, the girl who sat inside the sack called out:

"I see you! I see you!"

"The deuce you do!" said the troll. "Then you must have plaguy sharp eyes," for he thought all the while it was the girl inside the mountain who was speaking. He didn't dare so much as to peep into the sack again, but carried it straight to her mother as fast as he could. And when he got to the cottage, he threw it in the door.

"Here you have food from your daughter; she wants for nothing," he said.

Now when the girl had been in the mountain awhile longer, she did the very same thing with her other sister. She put her head on her shoulders, smeared her with ointment out of the flask, brought her to life, and stuffed her into the sack; but this time she crammed in also as much gold and silver as the sack would hold, and over all laid a very little food.

"Oh, please; oh, dear!" she said to the troll. "You really must run home to my mother with a little food again; and mind you don't look into the sack."

Yes, the troll was ready enough to do as she wished, and he gave his word, too, that he wouldn't look into the sack. But when he had gone a bit of the way, he began to think the sack got awfully heavy, and when he had gone a bit further, he could scarce stagger along under it. So he set it down, and was just about to untie the string and look into it, when the girl inside the sack called out:

"I see you! I see you!"

"The deuce you do!" said the troll. "Then you must have plaguy sharp eyes of your own."

Well, he dared not try to look into the sack, but made all the haste he could, and carried the sack straight to the girl's mother. When he got to the cottage, he threw the sack in the door.

"Here's food from your daughter; she wants for nothing," he said.

So when the girl had been there a good while longer, the troll made

up his mind to go out for the day; then the girl shammed to be sick and sorry, and pouted and fretted.

"It's no use your coming home before twelve o'clock at night," she said, "for I shan't be able to have supper ready before—I'm so sick and poorly."

But when the troll was well out of the way, she stuffed some of her clothes with straw, and stuck up this lass of straw in the corner by the chimney with a broom in her hand, so that it looked just as if she herself were standing there. Then she hurried home, and got a sharp-shooter to stay in the cottage with them.

When the clock struck twelve, or just about, home came the troll.

"Come with the food," he said to the straw-girl. No, she didn't answer.

"Come with the food!" roared out the troll again. "I am hungry." No, she didn't answer.

"Come with the food!" roared the troll the third time. "Listen to what I say or I'll wake you up."

No, the girl stood just as still as ever; so he flew into a rage and gave her such a kick that the straw flew all about the room. But when he saw that, he knew he had been tricked, and began to hunt everywhere. And at last, when he came to the cellar and found both the girl's sisters missing, he soon saw how the cat jumped, and ran off to the cottage, saying: "I'll soon pay her off!"

But when he reached the cottage, the sharp-shooter fired off his piece, and then the troll dared not go into the house, for he thought it was thunder. He set off home again as fast as he could lay legs to the ground. Just as he got to the trap-door, the sun rose and the troll burst.

Oh, if only one knew where the trap-door was! I'll be bound there's a whole heap of gold and silver down there still!

The Three Aunts

ONCE on a time there was a poor man who lived in a hut far away in the wood and got his living by shooting. He had an only daughter, and she was both fair and pretty. As the mother had died when she was a child, and now she was half grown, the daughter said she would go out into the world and learn to earn her bread.

"Well, my daughter," said the father, "true enough, you have learned nothing here but how to pluck birds and roast them, but still you may as well try to earn your bread."

So the lass went off to seek a place, and when she had gone a little while, she came to the king's house. There she stayed and got a place, and the queen thought so much of her that the other maids got envious of her. So they made up their minds to tell the queen how the lassie said she was good to spin a pound of flax in twenty-four hours, for the queen was a great housewife and thought much of all kinds of handiwork.

"Well, what you have said you shall also do," said the queen; "but you may have a little longer time if you choose."

Now the poor lassie dared not say she had never spun in all her life, but she only begged for a room to herself. That she got, and the wheel and the flax were brought up to her. There she sat crying and ill at ease and was at her wit's end. She pulled the wheel this way and that, and twisted and turned it about, but she made a poor hand of it, for she had never even seen a spinning wheel in her life.

But all at once, as she sat there, in came an old woman to her.

"What ails you, child?" she said.

"Ah!" said the lassie. "It's no good to tell you, for you'll never be able to help me."

The Three Aunts

"Don't be too sure about that," said the old woman. "Maybe I know how to help you after all."

Well, thought the lassie to herself, I may as well tell her. And so she told her how her fellow-servants had given out that she was good to spin a pound of flax in twenty-four hours.

"And here am I, poor me, shut up to spin all that heap in a day and a night, when I have never even seen a spinning wheel in all my born days."

"Well, child, that's all the same," said the old woman. "If you'll call me Aunt on your wedding day, I'll spin this flax for you; and so you may just go away and lie down to sleep."

Yes, the lassie was willing enough, and off she went and lay down to sleep.

Next morning when she awoke, there lay all the flax spun on the table, and that so clean and fine no one had ever seen such even and pretty yarn. The queen was so happy over the nice yarn she had got that she was even fonder of the lassie than before. But the other maids were still more envious, and hit on telling the queen how the lassie had said she was good to weave the yarn she had spun in twenty-four hours. Again the queen said well, what she had said she should also do, but if she couldn't quite finish it in twenty-four hours, she wouldn't be too hard upon her, she might have a little longer time. This time, too, the lassie dared not say no, but begged for a room to herself, and then she would try. There she sat again, sobbing and crying, and not knowing which way to turn, when another old woman came in and asked:

"What ails you, child?"

At first the lassie wouldn't say, but at last she told her why she was so sad.

"Well, well," said the old woman, "never mind!" If you'll call me Aunt on your wedding day, I'll weave this yarn for you; and so you may just go to bed, and lie down to sleep."

Yes, the lassie was willing enough, so she went and lay down to sleep. When she awoke, there lay the piece of linen on the table, woven so neat and close, no woof could be better. So the lassie took the piece and brought it to the queen, who was very happy to get such beautiful linen and became even fonder of the lassie than ever before. But as for the others, they grew still more bitter against her, and thought of nothing but how to find out something to tell about her.

At last they told the queen the lassie had said she was good to make up the piece of linen into shirts in twenty-four hours. Well, all happened as before; the lassie dared not say she couldn't sew, so she was shut up again in a room by herself, and there she sat in tears and grief. But then came another old woman who said she would sew the shirts for her if she would call her Aunt on her wedding day. The lassie was only too glad to do this, and then she did as the old woman told her, and went and lay down to sleep.

Next morning when she woke, she found the piece of linen made up into shirts that lay on the table—and such beautiful work no one had ever set eyes on, and more than that, the shirts were all marked and ready to wear. When the queen saw this work, she was so happy at the way in which it was sewn that she clapped her hands, and said:

"Such sewing I have never had, nor even seen, in all my born days." And after that she was as fond of the lassie as of her own child, and she said to her:

"If you'd like to have the prince for your husband, you shall have him; for you will never need to hire work-women. You can sew and spin and weave all yourself."

So, as the lassie was pretty and the prince liked her well, the wedding soon came on. But no sooner had the prince sat down with the bride to the bridal feast, than in came an ugly old hag with a long nose—I'm sure it was three ells long.

So up got the bride and made a curtsy, and said:

"Good day, my aunt."

"Is that an aunt of my bride?" said the prince.

Yes, she was!

"Well, then, she'd better sit down with us to the feast," said the prince;

but, to tell you the truth, both he and the rest thought she was a loathsome woman to have next you.

But just then in came another ugly old hag. She had a seat so broad and so fat that she was just able to squeeze in through the door. Up jumped the bride in a trice, and greeted her with: "Good day, my aunt!"

And the prince asked again if that were the aunt of his bride. They both said yes; so the prince said, if that were so, she too had better sit down with them to the feast.

But they had scarce taken their seats before another ugly old hag came in, with eyes as large as saucers, and so red and bleared 'twas gruesome to look at her. But up jumped the bride again, with her "Good day, my aunt." And her, too, the prince asked to sit down. But he was far from happy and he thought to himself:

"Heaven shield me from the kind of aunts my bride has!" So when he had sat awhile, he could not keep his thoughts to himself any longer, but asked:

"But how in all the world can my bride, who is such a lovely lassie, have such loathsome, misshapen aunts?"

"I'll soon tell you that," said the first. "I was just as pretty as your bride, when I was her age; but the reason why I've got this long nose is that I have always been sitting and poking and nodding over my spinning, and so my nose got stretched and stretched, until it got as long as you now see it."

"And I," said the second, "ever since I was young, I have sat and shoved backwards and forwards on the weaving bench, and that's how my seat has got so broad and big as you now see it."

"And I," said the third, "ever since I was little, I have sat and stared and sewn, and sewn and stared, night and day; and that's why my eyes have got so ugly and red, and now there's no help for them."

"So! So!" said the prince. "I am glad I came to know this; for if folk can get so ugly and loathsome by all this, then my bride shall neither spin nor weave nor sew again in all her days."

Doll in the Grass

ONCE on a time there was a king who had twelve sons. When they were grown big, he told them they must go out into the world and win themselves a wife each, but these wives must each be able to spin and weave and sew a shirt in one day, else he wouldn't have them for daughters-in-law.

To each he gave a horse and a new suit of mail, and they rode out into the world to look for wives; but when they had travelled a bit of the way, they said they wouldn't have Cinderlad, their youngest brother, with them—he was good for nothing, they said.

Well, Cinderlad had to stay behind, there was no help for that, and he didn't know what to do or whither to turn. He grew so downcast he got off his horse and sat down in the tall grass to weep. But when he had sat a little while, one of the tufts in the grass began to stir and move, and out of it came a tiny white thing. And when it came nearer, Cinderlad saw it was a lovely little maiden, only she was so very small and tiny. She went up to him and asked if he would come down below and see the "Doll in the Grass."

Yes, he'd be very happy, and so he went.

Now when he got down, there sat the Doll in the Grass on a chair. She was so lovely and so beautifully dressed, and she asked Cinderlad whither he was going and what was his business.

So he told her how there were twelve brothers of them, and how the king had given them horses and mail, and said they must each go out into the world and find them a wife who could spin and weave and sew a shirt in a day.

"But if you'll be my wife, I'll not go a step further," said Cinderlad to the Doll in the Grass.

Doll in the Grass

Yes, she was willing enough, and so she made haste and spun and wove and sewed the shirt, but it was so tiny, so very, very tiny, not longer than so——long.

So Cinderlad set off home with it; but when he brought it out, he was almost ashamed, it was so small. Still the king said he should have her, and so Cinderlad set off, glad and happy to fetch his little sweetheart. When he got to the Doll in the Grass, he wished to take her up before him on his horse, but she wouldn't have that; for she said she would sit and drive along in a silver spoon, and that she had two small white horses to draw her. So off they set, he on his horse and she on her silver spoon, and the horses that drew her were two small, white mice. Cinderlad always kept the other side of the road, he was so afraid lest he should ride over her, who was so very small and tiny. When they had gone a bit of the way, they came to a great lake. Here Cinderlad's horse got frightened and shied across the road and upset the spoon, and the Doll in the Grass fell into the water. Cinderlad became very sad, because he didn't know how he could ever get her out again; but in a little while up came a merman with her, and now she had grown to the size of other human beings, and far lovelier than she had been before. So he took her up before him on his horse and rode home.

When Cinderlad got home, all his brothers had come back, each with his sweetheart. But these were all so ugly and foul and wicked, and they had done nothing but fight and pull their sweethearts' hair on the way home. And on their heads they had a kind of hat that was daubed over with tar and soot, and so the rain had run down off the hats onto their faces till they got far uglier and nastier than they had been before. When his brothers saw Cinderlad and his sweetheart, they were all as jealous as jealous could be of her; but the king was so overjoyed with them both that he drove all the others away, and so Cinderlad held his wedding-feast with the Doll in the Grass. And after that they lived well and happily together a long, long time, and if they're not dead, why, they're alive still.

K